Published 2013 by
A & C Black, an imprint of Bloomsbury Publishing Plc
50 Bedford Square, London, WC1B 3DP
www.bloomsbury.com

Collection copyright © 2013 Catherine Butler
Stories copyright © 2013 Katherine Langrish, Susan Cooper,
Liz Williams, Frances Hardinge, Frances Thomas,
Catherine Butler, Rhiannon Lassiter

The right of Catherine Butler to be identified as the compiler
of this work has been asserted by her in accordance with
the Copyrights, Designs and Patents Act 1988.

ISBN 978-1-4081-9304-4

A CIP catalogue for this book is available from the British Library.

Printed and bound by CPI Group (UK) Ltd, Croydon CR0 4YY

1 3 5 7 9 10 8 6 4 2

MIX
Paper from
responsible sources
FSC® C020471

Edited by

Catherine Butler

A & C BLACK
AN IMPRINT OF BLOOMSBURY
LONDON NEW DELHI NEW YORK SYDNEY

To Sue, Dru, the LJ crew,
Frances O'Sullivan, Ruthie too.

CONTENTS

INTRODUCTION

Catherine Butler

Winter has always been the proper time for telling ghostly tales. At this season Earth turns its face from the Sun, brooding on its own dark thoughts like a scolded child. If it slumbers, its dreams will not be easy.

In former days, when the winter hearth was both heat and light, the family would gather there to share stories. With the darkness lapping at their feet they told of ghosts and night hags, buccas and bogles, long-fingered lurkers in the reedy ditch. In speaking of such terrors they hoped perhaps to exile them to the realm of the unreal. That is a border the demons are always patrolling; its fences need constant repair.

Today, cocooned in light and glass, we smile at our superstitious ancestors. We have gone so far beyond them. Our windows do not whistle, the carpet is soft, our beds are warm and dry. The screens around which we gather, as they once gathered round the hearth, give us more than mere light. What need now of winter stories? We have physics to tell us what is possible. Psychology pins our nightmares like dead moths.

Yet… if we no longer fear the dark, why do we flood our rooms with manmade light? Why do we insist on music, chatter, anything rather than silence? Why this tinsel parade of distractions? What is it distracting us *from*?

THUNK!

As I ask myself these questions, the lights fail. The TV and computer screens go blank, and the fridge in the next room shudders to silence. Drawing back the curtain I see the night sky prickled with stars. The streetlamps too are dead.

"Just a power cut," I say out loud, although I am alone. "The lights will be back in a minute."

There is silence still, and nothing to fill it but the wail of a car alarm in the next street, and the sullen dreams of winter Earth.

Groping my way to the kitchen I fumble some candles and a matchbox. Dim shadows swoop across the room as I make fire. Just then there is a crash on the ceiling above my head, and at the same moment a pale and eyeless face presses itself against the window glass. The candle gutters in my shaking hand.

It takes only a moment for reason to step in. The crash is the clothes rack toppling over yet again, it assures me. The face is a blowsy summer rose, still hanging on the bush outside. It's perfectly explicable, says Officer Reason. Move along now, nothing to see. Reason is quickly on the scene – but fear is quicker, and I'm still looking back over my shoulder as I'm hustled away.

Soon the electricity returns, and the television flickers into life. The wheels of the world start turning.

Music beats and voices bleat. Advertisements shiver their feathers like peacocks.

Somehow, though, I cannot settle back into the distracted life. I leave the bright screen, lift the latch that keeps the dark out, and thrust my face into the snowy air. In the street I see the stealthy prints of cats and birds, and other creatures that I cannot name. The stars that prickled in the winter sky are still there, somewhere, beyond the orange streetlights. A few flakes of snow land on my cheek and nose. I hear the garden foxes screaming.

Shall we join them?

DARK

Katherine Langrish

I'm not afraid of the dark. It's streetlights I don't like, especially those glaring orange sodium lights. Have you noticed how strange they make people look, on the street at night? How their faces go pale and bloodless, and their clothes turn a dark, dirty grey, no matter what colour they really are? Have you noticed how hard it is even to see people – because the streetlights make them the same no-colour as everything else – as if they aren't really there at all, just moving shadows?

There's no such thing as colour. All those bright reds and blues and greens we see in daytime are only wavelengths. What shows up under the orange streetlights is just as real as what you see in daylight.

Maybe more real.

The year I turned eleven, the year I started at Larkhill Road Comprehensive – which I still secretly thought of as 'the big school' – was the year Mum caved in and got me a dog. She didn't *say* she got Chips to make up for Dad walking out on us, but I knew she had. I'd been begging for a dog for ages. I argued that it would be easy to exercise him: the park was only ten minutes away, and even closer, halfway down the hill, we had the old cemetery; lots of people walked their dogs in there. But she always said, "Dogs need company, Tim, and we're out all day, it wouldn't be fair." And I could see her point. It made me sad but I could see it, because the sort of dog I wanted – *longed for* – would have been a *big* dog. A big *muscular* dog you could wrestle and run with, Labrador-size, or maybe a bull terrier or even an Alsatian. There was no way a dog like that could be left at home for hours at a time.

I hated my first term at Larkhill. We got split up into different classes, and all my old friends seemed to find loads of new mates, and I got left out. Maybe I didn't try. I was missing Dad – and hating him for leaving us – and hating Mum quite often too, for not being, I don't know, *prettier*, or *nicer* to him or something, so that he'd have stayed. It was scary, how much hating I was doing. It left me exhausted and miserable. I didn't know myself any more. I didn't know who any of us were, now we weren't all together, like we used to be. I sat by myself on the school bus, and if anyone *had* to sit beside me they'd twist round and talk to their mates across the aisle while I stared out of the window. I might as well have been invisible.

But I wasn't. Being unhappy gets you noticed in the wrong way by the wrong people. Miles Bennett was the worst. He was in Year Ten, he was twice my size, he smoked and swore and shouted at the girls, he travelled on the same bus as me every day and got off at the same stop, and he was the one who started calling me Timid.

"Hey, Timid!" he'd say. "You stink. I can smell you from here. It's the stink of fear, isn't it? You scared of

13

me, huh? You scared?" Then he'd grab my bag and empty it out on the floor, or chuck it to his friends at the back of the coach where I couldn't get it. I didn't tell Mum. If Dad had been at home I might have told him – I might – but not Mum. I just couldn't.

She knew I was miserable, though, because one afternoon towards the end of October, just before Hallowe'en, she was waiting for me when I got home. She flung open the front door and said, "Surprise!" And there, peeping out from behind her legs, was a small spaniel with a speckled white coat, dark brown ears and a patch on his back. I stopped dead.

"What's this?" I said.

"It's a dog," said Mum, laughing but looking edgy. "Isn't he sweet?"

"You said I couldn't have one."

"I changed my mind. He's a rescue dog. I thought, well, if I walk him in the morning and you walk him after school… Go on – say something to him."

"What's his name?" I said, gulping. At last I had a dog! But she'd chosen him without me, and he wasn't the sort of dog I'd wanted. Bitter disappointment was flooding my veins.

"He's called Chips," said Mum, watching my face, "but you can change it if you like."

I didn't want to change his name, I wanted to change *him*. I called, "Chips, Chips," and held out my hand. The dog crept forward, tail tucked between his legs, and rolled over submissively. He didn't seem to have any spirit.

"Here's his lead," said Mum. "And look, a dog whistle! If you want to let him off, you can call him back with this." I took it and blew. No sound came out, but Chips sat up as if someone had kicked him.

"It's too high for humans to hear," said Mum. "Why don't you take him for a little walk?" I could see I'd have to. I clipped the lead to his collar and Mum handed me a small roll of poop bags. "You may have to clean up after him. I got you these."

She'd thought of *everything*.

"Yay," I said. "Thanks, Ma. Great present!" That misfired. It was meant to sound ironic, but it came out plain nasty.

Mum's face went stiff. For an awful second I thought she would cry. Then she just looked tired. "I've given you a *dog*, Tim. You claimed you wanted one, and now you've got one. Maybe he's not what you imagined, but he's the right size for us, and he's a lovely little fellow. Go on, take him out and get to know him."

I set off sullenly down the road, Chips scuttling at my heels. Every time a car went past, he flinched. When a bus rolled by, he leaped across in front of me and nearly tripped me up.

"Stupid dog!" I yanked his lead, and he shrank down and cowered. I was being horrible, but I couldn't help it. I'd wanted a *big* dog, I'd wanted to *choose him myself*, and I'd never have picked a dog like Chips in a thousand years.

With Chips dodging about on the end of the lead, we went down the hill past the rusty railings of the old Victorian cemetery. I stopped at the iron gates and looked down the long path between the yew trees, wondering whether to go in. It would be the quickest place to take him. And, for the first time, Chips showed some interest. He pulled on the lead and whined softly, flicking his tail as if the dark and the quiet appealed to him. Perhaps he was a country dog. Perhaps he wasn't used to city streets.

I took a few steps in. But… it was after five o'clock, the sun had set. On the road behind me the streetlights were already coming on, with a pale barley-sugar glow. The cemetery was full of gathering dusk. There was nobody about. Far down the path, a tall obelisk stood out black against the twilight. Gravestones lined each side, inscribed in curly lettering with names and dates. *In Memoriam... In Loving Memory... Departed This Life...* Close to the gate was a tall pointed headstone bearing a single word.

DARK

I'd seen it before. I'd often wondered about it. Now – well, now I didn't feel like wondering. I spun around, pulling Chips away. I'd changed my mind. We'd go to the park instead. But when I got to the bottom of the hill, Miles and two of his mates were hanging around the bus stop.

I knew what would happen. If I glanced at them it'd be, "What you looking at?" If I pretended not to see them, it'd be, "Are you ignoring me?" They'd kick my ankles, jostle me into the road, spit on me. I was afraid of them.

If only Mum had given me a big dog! I'd have been all right then. I could have walked straight past and they wouldn't have dared to bother me. But all I had was Chips. He was a coward, and so was I. I turned to slink away, and Chips chose that moment, *that very moment*, to squat down. I tugged frantically at his lead, but he resisted, and by then it was too late. Miles and his friends surrounded me, grinning.

"What's this, Timid, got a little *doggie*?"

"Oops, look what he's done!"

"Don't blame the dog, Timid, we know it was you."

"Let's see you clean it up. Go on!"

I fumbled one-handed for the poop bags, tore one off, dropping the rest of the roll, and one of Miles' friends kicked it into the road where it snaked out, unrolling as it went. As I bent to clean up, Miles grabbed the lead and jerked Chips away from me. "Pick up the poop, Timid – *I'll* walk the doggie!"

Chips cringed and cowered, just as he'd done when *I'd* jerked the lead a few minutes ago, and all of a sudden I was hot with shame and hatred. Chips didn't deserve this – not from either of us.

I scrambled to my feet. "Let go of him! He's *my* dog! Give him back!" Miles threw the end of the lead at me, laughing. A car swerved past, with a honk. And Chips bolted up the hill.

Something exploded inside me. I hurled the freshly-filled poop bag at Miles. He jumped back with a yell, but I didn't wait to see if it hit him. I tore after Chips, who was pelting up the pavement ahead of me, much faster than I could go – his ears flapping, his white coat a dingy yellow colour under the streetlights – and then he vanished. When I got level with where he'd been, I saw what he'd done. He'd rushed through the iron gates into the cemetery.

I don't think I hesitated. I ran up the path after him, shouting, "Chips! Chips!" Dark yews loomed over me, and there was a sad, sharp smell of leaf mould and earth. Pointed headstones leaned this way and that. Chips was nowhere to be seen. I came panting to the place where the obelisk stood in the middle of a gravelled circle. The path split four ways, one leading straight ahead, the others heading uphill and downhill between trees and bushes.

"Chips, where are you? Chips!" Tears pricked my eyes.

Feet pounded behind me. Voices howled. "Where are you, Timid? We're gonna get you! We're gonna *kill* you!"

I jumped off the gravel circle, dodged behind a tall ivied headstone and crouched there as Miles and his friends skidded to a halt under the obelisk.

"I saw him a minute ago."

"He's hiding. We'll never find him in this lot."

"We don't have to. He's gotta come out soon, hasn't he? They lock the gates at six. We can wait for him outside."

"I'm gonna kill him!"

One of them laughed. "Good thing the bag didn't burst, Milesy. You'd'a looked good, decorated with –"

"I'm gonna kill him anyway," said Miles. "Look, there are two gates, yeah? You two go down to the one on the bottom road, in case he goes that way. I'll watch the one we just used. If he comes out your side when they lock up, bring him round to me." He raised his voice. "Timid, you zombie! I know you can hear me! You got fifteen minutes to get out before they lock the gates. We'll be waiting for you!"

They crashed off in different directions. I huddled down in the wet ivy, thankful for the dark camouflage of my navy school sweatshirt. My phone buzzed. It was a text from Mum.

Where r u? Tea in 15 mins ok?

I was hiding in damp bushes, behind a gravestone. I'd lost Chips. The cemetery gates would be locked in fifteen minutes. Less. And when I came out, Miles Bennett was going to kill me. I texted:

With chips in park. Might be bit late.

Ok have fun. Love u.

I'd had a dog, and I'd lost him. And I *deserved* to lose him – but Chips didn't deserve to be lost. I didn't dare call him any more, or Miles would hear me. I imagined Chips, alone and terrified somewhere. He wouldn't know how to find his way home. He didn't even know he *had* a home. Nearly crying, I shoved the phone back in my pocket, and my fingers touched something cold and hard.

The dog whistle! Miles wouldn't be able to hear it, but Chips would: I'd already seen the way he sat up the first time I used it. I sprang out of the bushes and ran to the obelisk at the crossways, where I could see down all four paths. I set the whistle to my lips and blew. I could hear nothing, but it felt powerful. I could feel the resistance of the air as I blew. I could sense the signal speeding out in all directions, a piercing summons.

When I stopped blowing, the air seemed charged, electric. My skin prickled up in goosebumps. And the cemetery felt, I don't know how to describe it – disturbed. Aware. As if, in a radius all around me, things had suddenly lifted their heads and looked my way.

I didn't quite like it. My heart beat hard. The cowardly half of me wanted to run; the other half wanted to stay and wait for Chips. And I was full of anxiety about the time. It must be nearly six. What if I got locked in? But Chips, Chips…

Then I saw with relief that after all I wasn't alone. Halfway down one of the paths, a late walker was coming slowly up out of the dusk towards the obelisk. I wasn't the last person in the cemetery; there was still time. I blew the whistle again, two short blasts, and listened. Something rustled in the undergrowth. I choked back a cry – and Chips came hurtling out on to the path, lead trailing.

I fell to my knees. "Chips! Good dog! Oh you

good, good dog!" He tried to climb into my arms. We were both trembling. He licked my face with his warm tongue. I pulled him close, hugged him hard, and stood up. "Come on boy. Let's go."

Footsteps rasped on the gravel behind us. Chips looked round. His hackles rose and he growled. I turned in fright, but it was only the person I'd seen walking up towards the obelisk, a man in a shabby-looking coat and hat. I couldn't really make out his face, it was very dark under the trees, but there was enough reflected glow from the streetlights to see that he wasn't very big, and he looked old. I reckoned Chips and I could easily outrun him if we had to.

He nodded as he dropped into step beside me. "Found him, then. Your dog," he said after a minute. His voice was unpleasantly rough and low.

"Yes. Yes, I have! Did you see him running around?"

He shook his head. "Heard your whistle."

I put aside a stir of unease. He couldn't mean that. He must have heard me when I was shouting earlier.

We walked on. After a moment he said slowly, "Time you got out of here. The gates are locked every night, an hour after sunset."

So, I thought, *he must be the gatekeeper*. "I know," I said. "Are you coming to lock them?"

He didn't answer. Then he said, "I'll see you out."

I wasn't very keen on him, but he seemed all right, and besides, if Miles was waiting for me at the gates I'd have a better chance of getting away if I came out with someone official. It was really getting dark in the cemetery, but ahead of us the gates were still open. I could see the streetlights gleaming orange out there on the road, and cars passing.

"Nice dog," said the man.

"Thanks," I said, although Chips wasn't behaving well. He was pulling really hard, his paws scrabbling in the gravel, as though he couldn't wait to get to the road. "He's a bit nervous."

"Can't blame him," said the man. "Kept a lot of dogs in my time. Not now, of course." He had a funny way of talking, lots of pauses. "They don't like me now."

I was only half listening. We were nearly at the gate. And waiting on the pavement, peering in, was Miles. He spotted me. I saw his head go up.

The man stopped, and I stopped too, even though Chips was nearly throttling himself, galloping on

24

the spot, breathing in harsh panting gasps. I needed an excuse to hang around while the old man locked the gates. I wanted to keep him talking so Miles would know we were coming out of the cemetery together. The orange streetlight fell across the nearest gravestone, and lit in curling black relief the word:

DARK

I pointed at it. "That's funny, isn't it? Why d'you think it just says 'Dark?'"

The way he answered, you could tell it he thought was the stupidest question he'd ever heard. "Because that's what it is," he said. He paused. "Down there." And I was realising with an incredulous shudder that he wasn't being funny, that he *meant it*, when he jerked his head and added, "Go on. Out," and I was on the pavement under the streetlamp, and Miles Bennett was grabbing me.

Miles was grabbing me, but he wasn't punching or kicking me, or doing anything on purpose to hurt me, even though his fingers were digging into my arms. He was clinging to me like a drowning man, his face was pushed up against mine, and he was hissing in a high-pitched strangled whisper, "What is it? Oh God, what is it, *what is it*?"

I looked back. The old man was pulling the gates shut – from the inside. Bars of orange streetlight fell across his face, and I saw – both of us saw – he didn't have eyes.

Miles left me strictly alone after that. I'm fifteen now, and he's at sixth form college. Sometimes if I'm in town with my friends, I'll see him, but he'll cross the street to avoid me. I can tell he still remembers.

Chips is a great little dog. Cars and buses don't worry him any more. He sleeps on my bed at night, and Mum and I love him to bits. But I don't walk him in the cemetery, and I threw the dog whistle away. And I don't like orange streetlights.

They make everyone look dead.

THE PARTY

Susan Cooper

It was never quite clear whose idea it had been to have a party. Nobody in The Close had ever held a formal celebration of Hallowe'en before, though each of the six families laid in a healthy store of sweets and bars of chocolate every year. They knew that inevitably the youngest residents would appear in costume at each front door just before dark, shrilling "Trick or Treat!" with an apologetic, smiling parent dimly visible beyond. Last year, most admiration had gone to nine-year-old Freddie Thomson as a rotting mummy, accompanied, some said, by an ingeniously disgusting smell.

But this year, through some forgotten adult negotiation, there was instead an elaborate party at the Ransoms', and all the grownups were in costume as well. The Ransom children and their friends in The Close found this disconcerting. The focus of life in the weeks before Hallowe'en had always been on them, not on Dad's pirate costume or Mum's witch mask. Besides, Dad looked like an overgrown kid and Mum looked, well, embarrassing.

To distract the young, Charlie and Ruth Ransom had kitted out their barn for the party with every Hallowe'en-related game they could think of. (It was a fake barn, of course, since like almost every house in The Close it was only ten years old.) They had a barrel of water with apples floating in it, for bobbing-for-apples; they had more apples hanging on strings from the fake beams of the barn's roof; they had pin-the-tail-on-the-donkey; they had a row of pumpkins for a family decorating contest. There were many prizes to be won, all of them inside envelopes decorated with gold, silver or red rosettes.

"Money," Charlie had said to Ruth.

"Oh no," Ruth said. "No, no, no. A prize has to be something beautiful, something that shows we've taken trouble."

Charlie said, "Money."

"Money is *vulgar*."

Charlie rolled his eyes. "Ask Verity," he said.

Verity was their thirteen-year-old daughter.

"Darling," Ruth said to her, "if you won a Hallowe'en prize, would you like it to be a really pretty scarf, or some lovely ear-rings, or chocolates, or money?"

Verity said, "Are you joking?"

So the prize envelopes contained five-pound notes. Sometimes more than one. The residents of The Close were a prosperous group, and Charlie Ransom, a commodities trader, managed somehow to appear more prosperous than most whatever the state of the national economy. The same could be said of his neighbour and close friend Julian Hogg, who happened also to be the property developer who had erected The Close in the first place.

On Hallowe'en the Hoggs were the first guests to arrive at the Ransoms' door, at the top of the handsome marble steps, between the gleaming marble pillars.

"Trickatreat!" screamed six-year-old Tristram Hogg, a diminutive Spider-Man, as the front door opened. He rushed forward, brandishing his red plastic loot-bag. Then he stopped, and stood very still.

The door had been opened by a bent, truly hideous hag, with long grey hair wisping round a drooling mouth and bristly chin. Behind her was darkness, lit only by a dim red bulb.

Tristram backed away, reaching for his mother.

"Come inside, my dear," croaked Mrs Ruth Ransom. Then she gave a girlish little giggle, behind the awful immobile face.

Shirley Hogg, tall and slinky in a low-cut purple dress of a design worn by a certain TV presenter, shifted her cowering son to one side and embraced the hag. "Brilliant, Ruthie," she said.

Little Tristram Hogg breathed again. Slowly, he managed to smile. "Mrs Ransom! You're *super ugly*!"

"And the ugly lady must pour me a drink instantly," said his mother, "if I have to look at that face all night."

Up the long driveway came the next elaborately masked family, to gather in the dimly lit barn hung with strands of filmy plastic cobweb, and the party became loud and happy, as the children bobbed for apples and carved grinning mouths into pumpkins that nobody would ever eat. Soon three other sets of Close neighbours had arrived, the Thomsons, the Macaulays and the Fothergills, in costumes ranging from a caveman to a rap star. The caveman, dressed in two sheepskins, was Mr Macaulay, who believed improvisation was more virtuous than buying, and who had impressive muscles to display.

Julian Hogg snatched a triumphant bite of one of the hanging apples, having craftily chosen to become a bulging-eyed frog with a mask that covered only the top half of his face. He was wearing a green velvet jacket whose colour exactly matched the shade of the frog mask; his wife had spent weeks shopping for it. Julian Hogg had a talent for persuading people to give him what he wanted.

He said to Charlie Ransom, chewing, "No Mrs Wallace yet?"

"She said she'd come," Charlie said.

"I need to talk to her. For my Belgians it's very nearly a done deal. Are you sure your Swiss friend will be in on it?"

"Guaranteed."

They looked at each other, the frog and the pirate, and raised their glasses silently.

Mrs Wallace was a very different person from the other residents of The Close, and her house was very different from theirs and about four hundred years older. It was the original manor house of the estate which Julian Hogg had bought from Mrs Wallace ten years earlier, after her husband had died and left her with a great deal of property and no money. There were no Wallace children to hinder the sale. Julian had agreed that Mrs Wallace should be allowed to go on living in the manor for the rest of her life, and on the many acres surrounding it he had built the handsome houses of The Close, including his own. Mrs Wallace's only remaining possession was an ancient thirty-acre stretch of woodland known locally as Hunter's Wood.

Now Julian Hogg wanted that woodland too. He had enlisted two partners from Europe, and developed exquisitely detailed plans to cut down all the trees and build an American-style shopping mall. With three major towns a few miles away, Hunter's Wood was the perfect site. They would call it Castle View, for the distant outline of Windsor Castle on the flat Berkshire horizon. Mrs Wallace seemed unaccountably hostile to the scheme, but Julian was confident that the money would bring her round.

Shrieks of laughter erupted from the room behind them, where a Hallowe'en game was in noisy progress. Julian's son George, totally hidden inside his expensive Darth Vader suit, came tugging at his father's arm.

"Dad, Dad – it's your turn – feel inside the box! Come on, tell us what you feel!"

Julian joined the cheery circle, noting with satisfaction the difference between his family's impressive Hallowe'en outfits and the home-made masks of the principled Macaulays. George directed his father's hand to the hole in the black-draped box on the coffee table, and Julian dutifully reached inside.

"It's awful!" hissed Freddie Thomson, giggling. "It's really disgusting!"

Julian groped, and felt. *Olives*, he thought. *Some things never change. Olives in olive oil.* He made a revolted face, and a suitable sound to match.

"Eeeuw!" he said. "Eyeballs! Cats' eyeballs!"

The children happily shrieked in triumph, and then it was Charlie Ransom's turn, his daughter having forgotten that he was the one who had opened the tin of cocktail sausages that he would soon identify, shuddering with horror, as babies' fingers.

But just as he began, there was a disturbance at the front door: a sudden eruption of unexpected music, drowning out the soft background pop oozing from the stereo. It was live music, a high, lively sequence of notes played on a pipe and a stringed instrument that most of them had never heard before, and in from the front hall came two tall dancing figures dressed in chequered orange tights with black face-masks across their eyes: two Harlequins, playing a tabor and a lute.

Charlie Ransom's wife was calling him from the door, and in her voice he heard a faint note of panic.

"Charles! Mrs Wallace is here!"

But already everything had stopped, everyone had turned, entranced, to see the happy Harlequins – and the tall lady at the door, allowing James Macaulay to take her cloak. Part of her height was her eighteenth-century wig, a high pile of curls above a brilliant, elaborate long dress, and in her hand was the stem of an astonishing brocade face-mask studded with glittering stones. She held the mask over her face and reached out a graceful hand to Ruth Ransom and her bristling chin.

"Happy Hallowe'en, Mistress Witch!" said Mrs Wallace. "My nephews brought you some music!"

The Harlequins had effortlessly taken control of the room; the children loved them, copying every move as they danced round the room, playing. All the games were forgotten, even the babies' fingers.

Then for a moment the music stopped. The Harlequins paused, looking back at the front door. Mrs Wallace had her hand on the shoulder of one more figure, swathed in a black hooded cloak.

"And one more Hallowe'en friend!" Mrs Wallace said warmly.

"Allow me," said James Macaulay politely, reaching round for the black cloak – and as the hood fell back, the whole house seemed suddenly gripped by a deathly chill. The Hallowe'en mask inside the hood was an appalling face of vicious evil, deeply lined, the mouth curled in a snarl, the eyes glaring. Its malevolence was more powerful than any monster mask they had ever seen, perhaps because its lines were so human.

They all stared. It was an ancient, twisted, baleful face, and on its forehead were two stumps, bleeding. For a moment, everyone in the room was afraid.

Julian Hogg stood motionless, feeling as though an icy hand had gripped him by the back of the neck.

The smallest Fothergill child began to cry.

At once the Harlequins began their music again, a cheerful, jaunty tune. The man in the mask, a dark figure in black jeans and turtleneck, bent his terrible head towards Mrs Wallace in a little bow, and they began to dance. The tension in the room dropped at once, and the children began their capering again.

Julian Hogg shook his head, bemused, and went to find himself another drink.

The room filled with music and laughter; it was a happy Hallowe'en. After a while the lights dimmed, and the hosts, the witch-hag and the pirate, brought in a bowl of fruit punch flickering with little flames. There were glass cups to be dipped into the punch, and straws for those people forced to drink through a hole in a rigid mask. The straws were very popular; they glowed in the dark.

The children clustered round the punch-bowl, reaching for straws. Mrs Wallace and her partner paused beside them, and she dipped a cup into the fruit punch and drank. Then she carefully fitted a straw through the cruel snarling mouth of her friend in the twisted mask, and held up a cup so that he could drink too.

The children watched, warily.

Freddie Thomson was not a rotting mummy this year, but a unitard skeleton. He was lost in admiration, gazing up at the man's head. "That's the best monster mask I ever saw. Where'd you get it?"

"Not a monster," said the man, removing the straw from the hole in his mask's awful unmoving mouth. His voice was husky, with an accent that sounded vaguely West Country. "It's Herne. You know Herne."

"The ghost in Windsor Great Park," said Verity Ransom, who knew everything. She was a ghost in floating white silk, with a feathery white mask across her eyes. "Herne the Hunter. He haunts a big oak tree. But he had antlers."

"I had antlers," said the man in the mask. He gave his head a little jerk, and a drop of blood from one of his forehead stumps flicked on to Verity Ransom's ghostly white silk.

"How do you *do* that?" said Freddie Thomson in awe.

Mrs Wallace said, "The Great Park story is more recent, Verity. This is a much older legend, from our own old wood, Hunter's Wood. Haven't you heard it? A woodsman cut off Herne's antlers, long, long ago, so Herne's ghost protects the trees from anyone else who tries to cut them down. Whenever those ancient trees are in danger, his stumps bleed, and they tell him to come after the attacker."

"And he comes," said the masked man softly. "Oh yes, he comes."

He bent his knees a little, so that his terrible head was at the same level as the children's heads, and he turned, slowly, facing them one after another.

Mrs Wallace said, "I wouldn't want him coming after me, would you?"

The children were backing away. "No!" said a small Fothergill devil fervently.

Blonde Mrs Fothergill, an outsize Alice, reached for the little boy's hand. She said reproachfully to Mrs Wallace, "You know, I really feel – "

The man in the mask turned his face to her, with its wide yellow eyes and glistening wounded forehead.

"Herne the Hunter," he said in his soft husky voice. "When there is danger, he comes hunting, and none can stop him."

The small Fothergill made a whimpering noise.

Verity Ransom said in her high clear voice, "Don't be frightened, Petey. It's just Hallowe'en. That nasty old witch over there is really my mum, you know that. And this is just a Herne mask – look, you can see the string."

She pointed to the neck of the man in the mask.

Freddie Thomson peered critically at the neat bow of tape just visible in the man's dark hair.

"Yeah, there it is," he said. "And I can see a fold where the mask doesn't quite fit."

The man in the mask chuckled, in a totally different voice. "Darn! I've got to be more convincing!" And he gave a high screech and dived at the children around him. They scattered, howling happily, and the chase became a game. The Harlequins joined in, still playing, and the party was back in full swing.

Mrs Wallace found Julian Hogg's chunky green-clad form at her side.

"Good evening," he said. "So nice to see you. It's Julian, inside this froggy outfit. I'm hoping you and I will come to a mutually profitable agreement later this week. Your lawyers have heard all the details from my people, of course."

Mrs Wallace held her brocaded mask up to her face, and her eyes glinted at him through it.

"You know my feelings about Hunter's Wood," she said. "They go back a very long way. Those great trees are ancient, beyond counting. The wood is a powerful place, not to be touched. Time keeps it."

"But times change," Julian said genially. "And people change. We have to think of the future, Mrs Wallace."

"Yes, I've done that," Mrs Wallace said. "I spoke to my lawyers. I intend to give Hunter's Wood to the National Trust, to be preserved for the people and the ages."

Below the bulging green eyes of his frog mask, Julian Hogg's thin-lipped mouth tightened. Then he smiled.

"Come now," he said, "we can't have National Trust tourists parking up and down the borders of The Close."

"I'm sure that won't happen," said Mrs Wallace. "The Trust is very discreet and careful. And they will take very good care that nobody cuts down the trees of Hunter's Wood." She lowered the stem of her mask for a moment, looking at him over its glittering edge.

"Not even you, Julian Hogg."

Julian said, "You're forgetting that I own the Manor House."

"In which I have the legal right to live for the rest of my days," Mrs Wallace said peaceably.

"Indeed," said Julian. "But the agreement doesn't specify how much of it you occupy. If I can't buy Hunter's Wood, I shall be forced to convert the manor into an apartment building. And you'll find yourself living the rest of your days – legally – not in a splendid spacious house but in a one-bedroom flat."

He gave her another smile, and this time it was unpleasant and triumphant.

The Harlequins' music jingled on, and the children hopped to and fro.

"You are not a gentleman," Mrs Wallace said.

"Perhaps not," said Julian. "But I'm an excellent businessman."

Mrs Wallace gazed into the slits in the bulbous green froggy eyes of his mask, for a long moment.

She said, "You are. And luckily, so is a friend of mine."

She raised her brilliant fantastical mask to cover her face again, and turned, and in the same instant the room fell silent, because once more the Harlequins stopped playing.

"Aaaaaaw," said the children, who had been enjoying their cavorting. But the two Harlequins each gave them a little bow and followed Mrs Wallace, who was sweeping towards the front door.

Mr Macaulay, stationed near the coat-rack, helped to drape her heavy silk cloak round her shoulders, and she smiled at him. Then she left, as the Harlequins opened the front door, and they all went away past the marble columns, down the marble steps.

Out of the crowd of dancers came the man in the appalling mask, following them. "Thank you!" he called to the witch-face of Ruth Ransom, as he seized his hooded cloak from the rack. "Lovely party! Happy Hallowe'en!"

Julian Hogg had tried unsuccessfully to follow Mrs Wallace; he was standing beside the front door, in his green velvet jacket and his half-frog face. He put out a hand towards the man in the mask as he went by.

"I don't believe we were ever introduced," Julian Hogg said.

"Just a friend of Mrs Wallace's," the man in the

mask said. "A very old friend. A business friend, you might say."

He loped down the white marble steps into the darkness, and paused. Then he turned his head back toward Julian and the house, so that the light caught the appalling, immobile, vicious mask with the two bleeding stubs on its forehead. Julian found himself suddenly giddy, and he felt his fingers curl in against their palms, rubbing softly, as if they could still feel the greasy olives that might, or might not, really have been eyeballs. Somewhere in the night, or perhaps in his mind, he heard a thin high call like the note of a hunter's horn.

Still facing him, the man in the mask reached to the dangling straps behind his neck and pulled his mask away.

Nobody but Julian Hogg was there to see that the mask had been simply a copy of the dreadful face that was underneath. And the monstrosity of the real face was far more appalling because it was alive: now the glaring yellow eyes blinked, the twisted mouth moved its dark lips. For an instant Julian stared in horror at the terrifying malevolent sneer, and the stubs of horns dripping blood.

Mrs Wallace's old friend smiled at Julian. The smile was the worst thing of all.

"See you soon, Mr Hogg," he said.

Then he turned, and was gone.

THE GATES

Liz Williams

I didn't like our new home, but my mum said that it would grow on me. I wasn't sure about that. I thought that it was too flat, the hills a distant blur of blue. The village lay low and soggy. The grass in between the apple trees was puddled with wet and not only after it rained. It was late November now and everything was brown and grey. The trees looked as though someone had taken a black pen and drawn them against the sky. They were alder and willow and ash, Mum told me, and in the spring a man would go around with a machine and give the willows a haircut, until they looked like the ugly heads of old bald men. This was because willow grows too fast, she said.

"How do you know?" I asked her.

"Because I lived near here when I was a little girl, like you, Hannah. A bit younger, maybe – I was only ten when we moved away. I lived with my grandmother, your great-grandmother. She had a cottage in a village called Oddmore, which is on the other side of Taunton."

"Does she still live there?" I was curious. I hadn't known my nan, let alone a great-grandmother.

"No, she died years ago."

"Why did you live with her?"

"Because my mother couldn't look after me and then she died, too."

"Why couldn't she look after you?"

"She was ill."

"What was the matter with her?"

My mother sighed. "She had a problem with drinking."

"Oh." It was the first time we'd had this sort of conversation. I suppose it meant that I was old enough to understand, but I wasn't sure I liked that. "Did you like it there?"

"Yes, after a bit. At first I didn't. I thought the village was too small and nothing ever happened, especially after London, although we didn't live in a very nice part of the city. But there was a lot going on. I suppose these days you'd say I was a street kid."

"It's not like Bristol, either. Here, I mean."

"No, it's not, but you'll get used to it. It's a different kind of life."

I suppose it had worked before, for my mum, so she thought it might work again. But I was not sure that I would come to like it. The village was not a pretty one, but built of mainly modern houses. Ours was older, a proper cottage, but it was also damp and there were slugs in the kitchen in the mornings. Mum said they crawled up the pipe. I had to go to school on the bus but it was nearly the end of term and everyone already had their own friends. And they were all white: only one other girl was like me. I got tired of explaining that my dad's dad had been Jamaican, although actually they weren't horrible about it, just didn't seem to really get it.

So at the weekends I moped about the house, and eventually, on the third Sunday, my mother told me to go out and get some fresh air.

"You're always on that computer."

"I like the computer. I've got tons of friends on Facebook. And I've got to do my homework."

My mum looked amused. "You're not usually so keen on your homework."

"But Mum, this is for history. It's about the ancient Egyptians." I fingered the looped cross around my neck. My ankh: I never took it off. Sometimes I thought it was an anchor, as well an ankh. Linking me back to the past. My dad had left it with my mum when I was a baby, for me. It was silver. And Dad had loved anything to do with Egypt, she'd told me. He saw it as part of his ancestry: even though my grandad's family had come from Jamaica, the Egyptians had been a great African civilisation, he'd said. So I felt that the ankh was my link to him.

But it was no use protesting. I put on some wellingtons and went out through the gate into the orchard, and puddled about in the wet grass. There were apples, but something had chewed holes in them and they smelled cidery, which I didn't like. I went through the orchard, and found that the end of it led onto a field. There was a small brown pony, so I walked down the slope towards it and the long line of bushes at the bottom of the field. When I looked back, I was surprised at how invisible the village had become: I'd thought that all the houses and their gardens went back much further, but it was like being in the middle of nowhere. The bushes had long black thorns like iron nails and I didn't want to get too close. When I reached the place where the pony had been, it had gone.

I looked around. There was a hollow in the bushes. I thought the pony must shelter underneath them, so I ducked under and saw the pony some distance away, making its way through the maze of bushes without any hurry. At the bottom of the hill was a trickle of a stream only a few feet wide. I could follow it, I thought.

I could be an explorer.

Sometimes, I thought my dad was an explorer. Like Indiana Jones, in my mum's old movies. Off in the rainforest somewhere, talking to jaguars, or finding his way through a pyramid, looking for treasure. But inside I knew where my dad was: in the ground, long gone. My mum had said it was cancer but it wasn't. I'd found his certificate, which they give you when you die, and it said *overdose*. But it made me think all the more of my mum, that she'd tried to protect me, that it had been a struggle. My dad and my nan. It was the same thing, really.

The stream was winding, twisting through the thorn bushes. After a while, the thorn trees grew less thickly and after I'd climbed over a broken barbed wire fence, I came out into a small, bare valley, with slopes where the sheep had cropped the grass and gorse growing on the hill like sunlight. I kept following the stream, but I kept an eye on the sun, too, like a proper explorer would: it floated through the clouds like a ten pence piece. At one point, I climbed the hill, which wasn't really a hill, but just the slope of a field, and looked back; I saw the tower of the village church and I knew that as long as I could see it, I could find my way home.

Twenty minutes later and I could hear water. It was not like the trickle of the stream, but a steady rushing noise and it puzzled me: surely the hills were not steep enough for a waterfall? Then I came around a bend and saw that it was what's called a sluice. The stream was channelled, it poured through a gate like water out of a kettle into a much wider stream. Except that it wasn't a stream, really, but a canal: maybe fifteen feet wide, and very still. Past the place where the water flowed in, which was foamy and white, the canal looked like oil. The slope of the fields tailed off onto flat land, banked by willows. There was a path, but it was marshy and reedy, with the tall bulrushes like spears all along it.

So I followed the path. There was something about the canal, but I couldn't say what it was. I didn't like it and yet I did, at the same time, as though it was pulling me on. I couldn't help thinking about where it would end – maybe at the sea, although later I thought that this was stupid. It would probably join up with a river.

I walked for about an hour. I couldn't seem to stop, as though my legs were mechanically taking me forward like a machine, and I sang as I walked: it was a song that my dad had written for me. As far as I knew it was the only thing he'd left – that, my name, and the ankh of course.

Hannah and roses, Hannah and flames,
Whatever who knows is, Hannah's my name…

That's how it began, and maybe it was silly, but it kept me going.

I'd never walked so far before, even though I'd been used to walking up one hill and down the other and up again in hilly Bristol, there and back to school. But this was different: flat, and the canal didn't really change much, until I came to the gates.

When I saw them, I slowed down. At first, from far away, they appeared as a small black patch at the end of the canal. When I drew a bit closer, they looked like a doorway into the sky. They were huge, made of black metal, and they reared up above the motionless water of the canal. I could see some sort of mechanism – a wheel – set into the side of the gates, and probably this opened them. It did not look as if it had been moved for years. It looked painted shut, not rusty, just thick with black paint so that it shone, even though the sun was covered by the clouds.

I stood for a long time and looked at the gates. There didn't seem to be any way around them, unless you climbed up the bank, which was quite steep. I listened, but I couldn't hear any traffic, although there must be roads somewhere: I thought I was near Highbridge and that wasn't far from the M5: you could hear the motorway from a long way away. Maybe it was so still because it was a Sunday.

A twig snapped and I turned. There was a man standing behind me. He made me jump, and for a moment, my heart banged in my chest. But he was old. He had a walking stick and in the brambles was a little old dog like a piece of a hearthrug. He had come down the slope: now that I looked more closely, I could see a tiny path.

"Afternoon," he said. He sounded quite posh, like a retired teacher.

"I was looking at the gates," I said.

"The King's Drain."

"Sorry?"

"It's called the King's Drain. It's a sluice. Do you know what that is, young lady?"

"Yes. They explained it in school. It's like a gate for keeping water in and out."

He looked pleased. "That's right. This one lets the water out at Highbridge. If there's a high tide, though, they close the gates, because otherwise too much water will come in from the sea and flood up."

"I saw a flood," I said. "When we came here from Bristol. It was all over the road."

He nodded. "Yes, that happens, sometimes. Most of this land is below sea level. That's why it's called 'Somerset'. Before they put in all these drains and gates, it was flooded all winter – you could only graze cattle in the summer, you see, so it was called the 'summer country'."

That made sense. "That's interesting," I said.

He waved the stick at the gates. "They're important, those. Keep the sea back. Well, I'd better be getting along or my wife will be wondering where I've got to."

He gave me the polite smile that some grown-ups give to kids and called the dog on. I waited until he had gone further down the path and then I saw him cut up through another little path and disappear. It wasn't that I hadn't trusted him, actually, but I felt like being on my own. I didn't want to leave the gates, but then it struck me that it would get dark soon and I didn't like the thought of being on the towpath when I couldn't see. So I went back, walking quickly and singing my dad's song under my breath, along the canal, and the stream, and the field. I could feel the gates all the way, though, over my shoulder. It didn't seem nearly as long on the way back: it doesn't, if you've walked somewhere twice, I've noticed.

"Did you have a nice time?" my mum said, when I got in. "I was a bit worried. You were ages."

"Yes. I went for a walk. But I took my phone." I showed her.

"Where did you go?"

"Along the canal. I met a man who told me about the sluice at the end."

She looked vague. "Oh, is there a sluice? I'd forgotten about the canal. It's only a little one."

"It's called the King's Drain."

"I can't remember which king it would have been."

"He said it was to hold the sea back."

And it was. But not just the sea.

* * *

That night, I woke up. I don't know what woke me. But my heart was banging against my ribs again, and I felt light, as though I wasn't real any more. I knew I had to go back to the gates.

Going out at night on my own was stupid, I know that. But it didn't feel as though I had a choice. I dressed, and then I let myself out of the back door and ran through the orchard, and down the field, and into the thorns.

There was a full moon and the sky was full of stars. I hadn't realised that there were so many. In Bristol, the sky is orange because of all the streetlights and you can only see a few, but now there were thousands of them. The moonlight cast sharp shadows; the thorn trees were blue and black. I'd been feeling a bit scared but now I was excited: it was like being out in a secret world, that no-one else ever saw.

Soon, I was at the canal. The light from the moon lay along the water like a path, a silver road, and the gates were at the end, but much bigger than they actually were, really huge, like a castle. I was still excited, but afraid, too, and I told myself I had to be brave. I followed the moon path, until the black gates loomed up in front of me and then I had to stop.

The light fell on the big wheel so that it was silver, too.

Open the gates. The voice was in my head; maybe I was going mad. But the thought didn't bother me.

"I don't know how."

The wheel will open the gates.

There was a ledge, on which someone could stand to turn the wheel. So I hopped onto the ledge and put my hands on it. I had forgotten to bring gloves and the metal was frosty cold. It hurt my hands, but to my surprise the wheel span easily, really quickly, as though the slightest touch would send it whirling. I lifted my hands and the wheel spun until it was round like the moon and the gates began to open. I jumped down from the ledge.

Within the gates, everything was black. I couldn't see the canal, or anything beyond and now I was really scared.

Go inside.

"I don't want to."

You must. And I felt my feet taking me forwards into the blackness.

As I did so, however, I saw that there was a tiny light, a little spark like a candle. It was as though there was a very small figure, carrying a tiny lantern, walking towards me.

"Who's there?"

No answer.

"Who is it?" My voice sounded very small, too. Then the lantern flamed up and someone was standing in front of me, man-height. His skin shone in the light from the lantern and it was like the old mahogany chest of drawers that my mother had in her bedroom, whenever she polished it. There was a black cotton cloth around his hips and the gleam of gold. When I looked up, I saw that he had a dog's head, like a Dobermann: long and dark-furred. His eyes had a little spark. I ought to have run screaming but all the fear drained away from me, as if out of a sluice.

"Who are you?" I said. But I knew. Anubis, the Egyptian god of the dead. The one who guides souls home.

"They're waiting for you," he said. I don't know how he spoke, out of that dog's face, but he did. It was the voice which had been talking to me. Without waiting, he turned as if he expected me to follow him and walked into the darkness. So I did.

I think there was water, still, but I couldn't be sure. We walked for a short distance and sometimes it was as though the walls were metal, like bronze, and sometimes they were stone. At last the man with the dog's head turned and said, "We are here. Do not speak unless someone speaks to you. And tell the truth."

"Okay." I wasn't going to argue. I saw another door beyond his shoulder and then he opened it and guided me through.

I don't remember a lot about the place beyond that. It was high, like a big cathedral, and it would have been dark except that it was lit by torches along the walls. There were people sitting on enormous stone thrones and I couldn't see any of them clearly, but their skin was different colours – I don't mean white or black or mixed like me, except for the dog-headed man, but blue and green and red, as if a child had coloured them in. They looked Egyptian, too: I knew they were gods, but the thought was too big to handle.

At the end of the room was a pair of scales, the size of a house. They were almost too huge to see, although I did wonder whether I myself had simply become very small. I still don't know. In one of the pans of the scales, the left-hand one, there was a feather, as long as I was tall, curling and white.

In front of the scales sat a shadow. It was the size of a normal man, and it sat quite still, with its hands on its knees.

"Do you know who this is?" a voice said.

I couldn't tell who was speaking.

"No."

"His name is Zachary Upson. Do you know that name?"

I felt as though I'd suddenly stepped onto a ledge that was too high. I said, "Yes. He's my dad. *Was* my dad. His name was Zachary but my mum says everyone called him Bardy because he liked writing songs and his mum was Irish. Where bards came from," I added, in case, being Egyptian, they didn't know. My fingers closed around the ankh at my throat.

At that, the shadow lifted its head. I didn't remember my dad but I'd seen photos and a video that my mum had taken, when I was still a baby. So I knew it was really him, but he looked very young. He *was* young, I suppose. He'd only been thirty-one when he'd died. I don't know why it had taken all this time for him to come here, but perhaps there was no time in this place.

"We're ready for the weighing," the voice said. I didn't know what that meant but I'd been told to keep quiet unless I was spoken to, and whereas I might have disobeyed my mum or a teacher, this was different. Then the voice started speaking again and it was a list of everything my father had done: how he'd nicked things as a kid, and gone on to stealing cars, then drugs. Using, but dealing as well, bringing misery into other people's lives. I listened and I didn't say anything. It wasn't good. I hadn't known about any of it; my mother had kept all that from me and I was grateful, but also angry. I didn't know what to think.

As each of his crimes was spoken, a weight dropped, leaden and black, into the right-hand pan of the scales and it sank lower and lower. At last the voice finished – names, dates, convictions – and the sad-eyed dog-headed man turned to me and said:

"Now it is your turn, Hannah Rose. What do you know that is good, about this man, your father?"

The trouble was, he'd gone off when I was still a baby. Hadn't been able to cope, my mum said. Left her completely in the lurch and she hadn't been able to go back to her own mum, because my nan was dead by then. She must have been so alone. And yet, Bardy was my dad, and here was his shade, looking at me with a hope in his face that hurt.

I said, "He gave me my name. Hannah, because it was his mum's name. And he left me with this." I held up the ankh and they all leaned forwards, as if to look at it more closely. "And a song. For me. He wrote it for me."

There in the hall, with the great torches flickering fire over the walls, I sang my song in a little quivery voice, and the shadow before me grew more solid and at the end of the room, the scales shuddered. Slowly, very slowly, the pan that held the feather began to sink, against the weights, until the feather came to rest against the floor and the black weights were no longer visible.

My dad's figure wasn't shadowy any more. It was filled with light and it became brighter and brighter until it was gone, but I could see that he was smiling. There was an opening in the air behind him, a doorway shaped like a cross with a loop at the top, like my ankh. He stepped through it and when he disappeared, the torches began to go out, one by one, and as the last one guttered I was in total darkness. I think I yelled, but the dark swallowed the sound. Then I saw that an eye was staring at me, a huge white eye, and a moment later I realised that it was the moon. There was no sign of the hall, or the great figures, or the dog-headed man. I was standing in front of the gates, but the sluice looked different. It was much smaller, and made of grey metal like the little sluice further down the canal. I could not see the wheel. I wondered whether the gates opened into other worlds, other lands of the dead, and my dad had gone to the one he loved best. But I knew that whatever the gates looked like, they were not just to hold back the sea.

If this had been a dream, I suppose this was the point at which I woke up. But it was not a dream. I was stiff and frozen, the reeds crackled with frost, the moon was on fire in the coldness of the sky, and the canal smelled of weed and water. I trudged home along the towpath, and sang my song as I went. The pony whickered to me when I came up the slope of the field. The orchard no longer seemed unfriendly, with things lurking behind the apple trees, and when I lifted the latch on the back door, the sky was already growing brighter in the east. There were flowers of frost on the windowpane. I did not go to bed, but sat in a chair by my bedroom window and watched the sun come up over the blaze of the world after the darkness of the night.

FLAWLESS

Frances Hardinge

When people stay in hotel rooms, they suddenly turn into toddlers. Weird, creative, screwed-up toddlers.

Let's smear jam on the wall! Let's leave apple cores in the drawers! Let's hide used nappies behind the radiator, so that they fill the whole room with the smell of cooked poo! Hello, whoever cleans this room! I've left you a surprise!

Maybe they think there's some hidden handle we pull to flush the room clean. But there isn't. The only 'handles' are Mum, 'Occasional Kev' from the village, and me. Kev's just Occasional and Mum has everything else to do, so cleaning is mostly my job, particularly during the school holidays.

Cleaning a room is like being that legend-guy who pushed a rock up a hill again and again. While you're scrubbing at the gribble, most of the time you can't even tell if you're making any difference. Nothing's ever perfect. Your eye adjusts. The closer you get to perfection, the better your gaze learns to pick out the stains and marks.

When I've finished a room, I always step into the corridor for a moment, taking in the spotted walls, the gingery time-stains on the mock-brass electric chandeliers. Then I enter the room again, and for one moment it *is* perfect. It gleams, like it's just been taken out of its packaging.

That never lasts. Next day there will be inexplicable bootmarks on the curtains, and somebody will have tried to cook soup in the kettle.

I don't know why they bother. After all, we already have a weird, creative, screwed-up toddler of our own.

Dill is two years old, and tall for his age – tall enough to reach door handles. He has a rubbery little mouth and big, wet blue eyes. He wants to hit everything in the world against everything else. If you don't let him, his eyes get wetter, and his scream goes right through your brain.

He's my brother and I love him. Of course I do. But sometimes loving him feels like just one more thing I do because it's my job.

He adores clean rooms. He rushes around them like some grimy, stumpy spirit of Undoing, throwing pot plants on the floor and stamping on biscuit packs. Once he left a toy truck in one of the teacups, with a live slug in the driver's seat. I'm not making this up. And he's two, so whatever he does is *my* fault.

Once I dared to suggest to Mum that maybe Dill was *too* hyper. But no, apparently he's just 'being a boy' and 'letting off steam'. I didn't ask what was supposed to happen to *my* steam. No, I just swallow it down, so that I can be the 'nice smiley girl at reception' and Mum's little helper.

Or at least I did until this winter, when the snows came and changed everything.

* * *

We're not exactly a winter destination. Our hotel is on the cliff path, with views down to Windmouth (fading spa town) on one side, and Creve (failing fishing village) on the other. From October onwards, the wind from the North Sea does its best to blow us somewhere more sensible inland. It always fails, but I'm rooting for it.

Low season means more free time for me, but this winter I spent every spare minute wrestling with my GCSE work. Mum didn't stop me, but whenever she caught me studying her face went neutral, and I knew what she was thinking. Mum has always wanted me to leave school after my GCSEs, and work in the hotel. Worse, I know it isn't just because she needs the help. *She thinks I'm wasting my time*. She doesn't think I'm smart enough to bother with university. She thinks I'd drop out, or waste three years of my life for nothing but a big, fat debt and an unclassified degree.

I didn't tell her how badly I was doing. I didn't tell her that my brain froze up whenever I tried to prepare coursework. Blank paper, blank screen. Time and again I lost the staring competition. A barrier in my head stopped me filling them with words. I might as well have tried to write across the sky. By December I was going spare.

The snow arrived one evening by stealth. First tiny ice-crumbs spiralled down, flecking my lashes and sleeves while I took out the rubbish bags. After dusk came small, soft tufts that melted on the sills and damp tarmac as soon as they landed. Then followed big fat flakes, blue with the late evening light.

Doors, windows, just a whirl of snow. Sorry, we are not receiving transmission from the world at present. You are between channels.

Next morning, when I peered out of the window of my attic room, the sheer beauty of the world outside knocked the breath out of me. There was thick snow everywhere, heaping up on the windward side of the cars and buildings. It hung over the edge of the cliff in a smooth, crazy, cartoon way. The sky seemed full of sun. The snow was so white you could feel it throughout your head, like toothache but without the pain.

For half an hour I sat there looking at it, completely happy. It was the white I'd been scrubbing to find under the chipped china and worn-out tiles. Perfect. Flawless.

Of course it didn't stay that way. Dog-walkers, hikers, postmen, delivery men, they all started to rut and spoil my beautiful snow. The buggies from the surrounding golf course took their usual short cut through our land to get back to their club hut, leaving deep tracks.

Dill had never seen snow properly before. He wanted to zigzag all over it, and fall in it, and throw it. Most of all, he wanted to *spoil* it. He seemed to find every pure, beautiful patch, and then take pleasure in stamping it into slush.

"Keep an eye on him," said Mum.

I took my history book outside, and leant against the footpath stile near where he was playing. I couldn't study, though. I had to watch Dill as he scuffed my gorgeous snow and warbled in a tooth-edgey falsetto. Suddenly the whole scene felt like The Symbol of My Life.

She must have come up along the coastal path behind me, but I didn't hear her approach. There was no soft, powdery huff, huff, huff of feet stirring snow. All I knew was that suddenly there was another figure leaning over the fence, watching Dill.

It was a woman in a pale blue coat, with silvery

fake fur around the neck and hood. I thought she looked Swedish, with her pale lashes and pure gold hair. Her face was tanned, but I wondered whether it was a skiing holiday tan, not a beach tan. I realised that I was blocking the stile and moved hastily, but she carried on staring over the fence.

I waited for the usual inane comments that Dill draws out of adults. *He's having fun there, isn't he? Wish I was his age.* But the silence stretched.

"He's my brother," I said. It was weird to start a conversation that way, but all I could think of to do was to answer the routine remarks that hadn't been made.

"Then can't you stop him doing that?" answered the woman, without looking at me.

Her tone held the suppressed frustration that I often felt when I watched Dill. When she glanced at me at last, her small frown melted away, as if my face had mirrored her own feelings.

"No," I said. "I can't. Mum lets him do whatever he wants."

Her irises were dark at the rim but silvery grey nearer the pupil. In contrast, her lashes were shockingly white. As we locked gazes, I felt the woman enter my head as a guest. She walked through the rooms of my mind, but disturbed nothing, trod no dirt into the carpets. She ran her fingertips along surfaces and examined them, then nodded approvingly.

"No," she said softly, "but you would if you could. He spoils *everything*, doesn't he?"

I flushed, and nodded. The 'steam' that had never been 'let off' filled me right then. For the first time somebody understood. The relief was painful.

"Some people do," the woman murmured. "They do not care how long others labour to create, to restore, to clean, to preserve – they must always mar. Destroy. Stain."

"There's nothing I can do about it." My voice sounded mangled and tearful.

"And if you could do something?" she asked softly. "Something to stop your brother spoiling anything pristine, ever again?"

"You mean, apart from throwing him off the cliff?" I gave a hasty-sounding laugh to show it had been a joke. Somehow it hadn't sounded like one.

She smiled. "Oh, nothing that drastic would be necessary."

I was starting to get a tingle-kneed feeling as if the precipice was much closer than it actually was, as if it had been inching towards us during the conversation.

"Yes," I said. "I'd like it if all the spoiling and breaking just *stopped*."

"Then bring him here," she said.

And I did. I walked over to Dill, my face burning, and a terrible warmth in my chest. I called him over. I picked him up. I walked back to the woman at the fence.

I didn't know what would happen. I would love to tell you that I thought it would be nothing terrible. But deep down I think I knew.

"What's his name?" she asked, giving him a smile bright as dewdrops.

"Dill."

"Hello, Dill." She leant over the fence, and kissed him on the forehead.

Dill's blue eyes widened, and he screamed. When the woman straightened, I almost expected to see her kiss seared into his forehead, but there was no mark. I set him down, and watched him stumble away with a feeling of shock and growing guilt.

I turned back to the woman, just in time to see her gloved fingers delicately plucking a small black bead from her mouth, as if she were discreetly spitting out a cherry stone.

"What did you do?" I demanded.

She did not answer. Instead, she touched the bead to a bracelet of similar beads on her wrist, where it joined their ranks, smoothly and impossibly. Then she turned and strode away, down the path towards Creve.

Watching Dill blunder towards the front door, I felt my heart lurch. His stubby feet were not sinking into the snow. He left no prints behind him.

* * *

I have guilt dreams sometimes. Dreams where I've killed somebody. I can't remember who or why, but I know that I've done this terrible thing I can't undo, and I just can't believe it. When I wake up, the relief is indescribable.

Walking into the house after Dill, I was filled with the guilt dream feeling. But this time I knew I really *had* done something terrible, and I wasn't going to wake.

Mum was on a ladder mending lights, her brown-and-grey curls scrunchied back. She grimaced when Dill ran wailing to the base of the ladder.

"Chloe, can you take him? Give him his colouring books."

Dill thumped my shoulders while I carried him to his play room, but he settled when I laid out his crayons and Disney colouring book. He loves colouring. It's the only time he's quiet. It's like a drug. He loves vivid shades, particularly reds and blues. He can't keep his scribbles inside the lines, but he tries. Mum says he's artistic.

And sometimes when I watch him colour, my mind is quiet too. I start to think that maybe he's just a fat little bottle bursting with… *stuff*. Energy and craziness that comes out in screaming and breaking, except when it can come out in red and blue.

Today was different, however. Dillon curled his fist around a red crayon, and drew it hard across Goofy's muzzle. Nothing happened. No colour, no mark, not even a dent from the pressure. He scratched it desperately to and fro, so hard that the page should have torn. It didn't. Goofy smiled back unblemished.

For a few seconds Dill could only croak, his mouth making rubbery, trembling shapes. Then his scream was like an earful of molten lead. I hushed him in vain, bounced him on my knee, and sang him songs. Big sister of the year. I felt like such a hypocrite.

As lunchtime approached, a new dread seized me. *What if he can't touch anything, including food? What if he can't eat?* Mum was too busy to fix Dill's lunch, so I took care of it, my heart hammering.

As it turned out, he *could* eat. Or at least, he could eat things I'd chopped, mashed or broken up for him. But he couldn't cut or chew things that were intact. His teeth couldn't dent biscuits. Grapes went into his mouth, then came out whole and glossy with spit.

I started to understand. The woman in the snow had promised that Dill could never spoil anything pristine again. So he couldn't affect anything pure, clean or whole.

He isn't going to die, I told myself. *It could be worse.*

But as I struggled through my lasagne, his future existence unrolled before me. What kind of life could he have if he could only eat food broken up by someone else? What would happen when he went to school? He would never be able to write, draw, sign his name – maybe not even type into a keyboard. He would never be able to open envelopes, jars, tins, packets. He would be a freak forever, sliding off the surface of the world like raindrops off waxed cloth.

* * *

By mid-afternoon the sky was dim as twilight, and more flakes were flurrying down.

I could still hear Dill's desolate wailing while I scrubbed floors, bleached toilets and scraped the lime off shower screens. Nothing I did was undone. No thrown orange juice beakers left sticky patches on the carpets. No jam murals appeared in the corridors.

I was tense all the while, knowing that any moment Mum would hurry to Dill to see what was wrong. She would take one look at him and *know*, using her extra-terrestrial mother-powers. And then I would hear her accusing voice calling for me…

But the hours passed, and she didn't go to him. After a while it started to creep me out.

She just went on working. His loudest screams made her frown, but in a distant, distracted kind of way.

When I brought him to the kitchen for dinner, I found that she had laid two places at the table, but hadn't brought out Dill's high chair. Dill ran over to her, yanking with desperation at her skirt, but she just stared down at him, as if trying to remember who he was. Then she walked away to the fridge, leaving him to topple and sprawl in her wake.

My blood ran cold. I went over and picked him up.

Dill. Dill, her angel. Her favourite boy. The one who had left a thousand marks upon her heart and memory – bruises and jam smears, tiredness creases and crayon hearts. Before my eyes, those marks were fading, like footprints covered by falling snow.

She was ceasing to care about him. Soon she would not remember him at all.

* * *

Dill's screaming stopped eventually, his voice worn down to a miserable, quavering croak. Mum's coldness seemed to break his world in two.

For once he *did* have a reason to cry, a reason I understood. Dill was finding out how it felt when your pain didn't count. Dill had fallen into my world, but he had plunged past me into the darkness and was still plummeting.

I spent what time I could with him, but disasters kept dragging me away. A pipe burst, flooding the cellar, and I had hardly finished dealing with that when I had to go out and shovel snow off the ornamental bridge so it didn't give. I brought Dill his truck and left him to play in the hall.

While I was shovelling, my mind spiralled through nightmares. What would happen to Dill when I was at school, if Mum forgot he existed? What if nobody ever cared if he lived or died? What if all the crazy *stuff* inside him could never get out through colouring or breaking or getting attention? Would he go mad? I thought he would go mad.

As those thoughts were going through my head, I looked up and saw the woman of the snows standing between our two pines, staring at me with a face like carved ice.

She wore a dress of furs, so white it merged into the surrounding snow. Her shoulders and long neck were bare, and her hair was loose. She was glaring at my shovel blade, embedded in her sweet, luminous snow. Somehow she seemed taller than before.

Dropping the shovel I ran towards her, but she melted amid the flurry of flakes, became a pattern of shadows amid the smooth snow hummocks. I stumbled around for a while, calling out, but she had vanished.

I came back to find Mum sweeping the step and the front door ajar. Dill's truck lay abandoned on the threshold. There was no sign of him.

"Mum – where's Dill?" I stared around at the thickening blizzard. "Did Dill come out here?"

Mum did not seem to hear.

"Come on in, Chloe," she said. "I'll go make us some cocoa."

I sprinted around the house, flinging open doors, but Dill was nowhere to be found. He must have wandered out past Mum, without her giving him a second glance. Now he was somewhere on the icy cliff paths, and there weren't even any tracks for me to follow.

* * *

I didn't try to reason with Mum, or call the rescue services. Even if they started searching for Dill, within minutes they would forget what they were doing, or stop caring. Instead I wrapped up warm, grabbed a torch and ran out.

For an hour I scrambled along the cliff paths, yelling Dill's name. Every shadow or half-buried stump looked like his sprawled shape. Every note in the wind sounded like his wail. Soon my feet and hands were aching with the cold.

The dangerous thing about despair is that it's the *kind* voice in your head. It's the one that says, *oh well, you tried your best. There wasn't anything you could have done. Time to give up.*

I couldn't give in. The voice was right, though, I wasn't going to find Dill this way. So I changed tack and went in search of *her*.

I knew where she would be. There's a broad, high headland where the ground is smooth and unbroken, a perfect laying ground for snow. It has fine views of the other heads as well, just the place for somebody who wants to admire their white, velvet-smooth domain.

Sure enough, when I huffed my way up the slope, there she was, standing at the highest point. Star-pure. Gleaming. All disguises cast aside. Something inside me quailed and bowed when I saw her. She made the snow looked dingy in comparison, and for a crazy moment I wanted to throw myself down and polish it, so that it was fit for her to tread.

She looked at me and smiled. I felt like a scuff mark on the world

"No," she said. The question I had not asked soured in my mouth. "No, I will not give him back his power to spoil. I am disappointed that you would ask it."

I swallowed hard. I stared around me at the lifeless purity of the scene. I thought of Dill and Mum. I found the smile I used in reception and spent a moment straightening it on my face.

"That's not why I'm here," I said.

She looked at me for a long moment. One of her eyebrows rose slowly. Perhaps she didn't believe me. Or perhaps I had her interest.

"You're beautiful," I said. "You're... *flawless*. I try so hard to be one of the people who make the world spotless. But... when I look at you, I see how grubby and clumsy I am. I want to be more like you. Whatever you took from Dill, can you take it away from me too?"

Her gaze felt cold as it touched my scruffy hair, red nose, frayed gloves. She smiled again.

"Very well," she said, and moved towards me.

As she drew closer, I kept my head bowed, breathing hard and forcing myself to stay still. She was two steps away, then one, and my skin was stinging with a terrible, blistering cold. Even with my gaze lowered, I could see her stooping to plant a kiss on my forehead...

... and at the last moment I ducked my head, and snatched at the bracelet of black beads around her wrist.

I yanked at the bracelet, and it gave. The beads sprang loose, but they did not tumble to the ground. Instead they whirled into the air and surrounded me, a swarm of wheeling black blobs.

The woman gave a thin sound of rage like a rising wind. It rose until the air shook, and I fled, half-blinded by the flurry of white flakes and black motes. As I ran, the beads pelted me, seeking exposed flesh. When they found it they clung and stung, burying their way into my skin. The more they did so, the less my limbs felt like my own.

I tumbled repeatedly, crushing shrubs. I put my foot through the bridge outside the hotel, and flung the front door open so hard its windows shattered. Then I blundered through the hallways and corridors, leaving mud, snow and blood from a cut hand everywhere I went.

Mum had no patience with me. Five minutes before, she had noticed that Dill was missing, and she had been searching for him frantically ever since. She was sure I must have left the front door open when I went out for my 'walk'. Fortunately we found his tracks in the snow, and followed them to his huddled, whimpering shape behind the shed.

Mum was so angry that she barely spoke a word to me for the rest of the night.

* * *

No. Things aren't back to normal. Not for me, anyway. Oh, Dill is much the way he used to be, and Mum's even more protective now after 'what nearly happened'.

But me? I'm hopeless.

I spoil everything. I can't make a bed without ripping sheets. I can't clean a window without breaking it. I can't join a conversation without dropping a big, fat spiked truth into it, like an anchor through the bottom of a rowing boat.

And when I sit down in front of a blank page or an unsullied screen, the words pour out. Thousands of them. All my fears and feelings and dreams and rage. I can't stop them.

I don't think I have a future in hotel cleaning. I don't think I'm a servant of the flawless any more. Some day perhaps I can return to something like my old self, but for now I can't.

For now I've got a lot of spoiling to do.

LOSERS

Frances Thomas

The best part of the day, Brad thought. The light was growing dull, and the school bus in its fug of misted windows slowly wove its way through narrow lanes, spiny bare hedges scraping against the window, everything cold and bleak outside, and waiting for him at home, hot tea and maybe a big peanut butter sandwich, or a wedge of homemade cake, the Rayburn stove filling the kitchen with warmth and the old dogs barking in the yard. English homework tonight, but he wasn't going to do that if he could help it, silly cow. Waste of time, school, his dad always said. It wasn't school learning that had got *him* the biggest farm in the valley, money stashed away, and the respect of all his neighbours. Teachers, said his dad, were losers, just like those daft folk in the cottage at the bend.

Thinking that made Brad sit up in his seat and look out for little Rhys, sitting two in front of him in his old yellow anorak, hunched up as usual. No doubt thinking of all the fun Brad was going to have when they reached that bend in the lane, halfway between his cottage and the farm, where no-one could see what you got up to. Oh how Brad looked forward to that bend in the lane!

Leesers Cottage, it was called, probably something from the mashed-up Welsh that got used round here, but of course his dad always called it *Losers*, and the name had stuck now, even in the village. They'd always been losers, from way back, folk who lived in that cottage. Stock got sick, crops failed, bankruptcies; one lot of losers moving out and another lot moving in. Then that story of the girl drowning herself. That was a long time ago, way before anyone could remember, but they still told the story. No-one knew why, but she drowned in the lake, down the Cae. The Cae his father wanted to have, only the old witch wouldn't sell. Just her and that Rhys, now, the current lot of losers. A hippy, Dad called her, with her long drippy hair and wooden necklaces. Only a bit of land left to Losers Cottage now, a few chickens and a few vegetables, what sort of a living was that? And whatever had happened to their old man? Walked out, his dad said, couldn't take being stuck with a witch like her, and that fool of a lad. Sometimes, she'd be at the mouth of the lane waiting for her boy as he got off the school bus, and there'd be nothing Brad could do about it. But mostly she worked, four days a week in the community centre in Llanwen. Brad's mother had never had to go out to work a day in her life. She knew what being a farmer's wife meant: stay at home, look after your menfolk, be there for lambing and haymaking, the important stuff. Not sitting all day on your backside in a stupid office, earning pennies.

With any luck, Rhys's mum wouldn't be there today at the lane, and Brad could plan what to do. Oh, you could have such fun without leaving a mark! He knew exactly how far to bend back an arm before it would crack and get you into real trouble, how long you could put pressure on a throat before the kid turned blue, how tight to make a Chinese burn. And, daft kid that he was, Rhys never even fought back, skinny little runt, with that pale face and big frightened eyes. Fact was, Brad was even doing him a favour, showing what it meant to be a man. Better find out now rather than later it was muscle-power got you where you needed to be in the world, muscle-power and making folk afraid of you, that was what counted, not book-learning.

And then there was all the fun you could have without laying a finger – that was the best. Suppose a fox got into your chickens at night – not that Brad could probably have achieved that, but he *said* he knew how, and the lad went paler than ever. Or that time he grabbed the lad's homework – all that neat writing! – and shoved it into a cowpat in the lane. And then how the lad had whimpered, really whimpered, when that old cat he was so fond of had come along, and Brad had said all the things he could do to it. Mind, he never would, really, the way the ugly mog had scratched him only time he tried to pick it up. Maybe he could set the dogs on it one day – Patch could be proper vicious, specially if you gave him a kick to egg him on – but probably it'd be too much trouble. Plenty of other things he could do to the lad without getting scratched to ribbons first.

The bus came slowly to a halt at the foot of Rhos Lane (see, even the lane was named after his dad's farm; it wasn't called Losers Lane, now was it?) and George the driver called out, "All right, lads?" Only Brad and Rhys got out here, half a mile of un-made-up road the school bus couldn't go up, though his dad managed perfectly well with his tractor and quad bike. That was another thing Rhys's mum was on about, couldn't he get the road made up, all that mud and ice in the winter, but his dad said, why should he? Let her pay for getting it tarmacked, stupid cow, if she was so keen.

Brad grinned at George as he stood up in the bus. Rhys stood up too, and with a wave of his arm, Brad generously let him get off the bus first; you'd think they were best of friends the way he behaved towards the lad in public.

"Mind how you go now," said George as he always did, and Rhys and Brad tumbled down the steps of the bus onto the grass verge and then on to the muddy lane. They stood and watched as the bus trundled off down the road and into the distance. After the warm fug of the bus, the December air was like an icy slap in the face; you could almost feel your eyelashes freezing up. This morning's heavy frost hadn't even melted, and the whiteness shimmered on the hedges and in the meadow, everything colourless and chill, only a few hawthorn berries blood-red against the grey. A river of ice ran down the edge of the lane; it had been there for days.

Then Brad turned to Rhys and said with a grin, "Aw*right*, kid?" Fact was, he hadn't quite decided what he was going to do to the lad today, but he had a few ideas, and by the time they got to that bend in the lane he'd have worked it out.

Rhys was already walking away. Brad called out after Rhys's narrow hunched-up shoulders, "Awright, then? Ready for some fun tonight, are we?"

Usually, this made Rhys cower even more and try to scurry away. But today something odd happened. For Rhys suddenly stood stock still in the lane, straightened his shoulders and turned to face Brad.

"You've got a big mouth on you, you know that, Brad Williams?"

For a moment Brad was so surprised that he went silent. What the heck did the lad think he was up to? Then he gathered his wits together, put his best menacing face on, and advanced on the kid. "You what?" he said, quietly. Always best to be quiet at first, like his dad always went when he was working up to get really angry.

And now he had to show that Rhys. And he wasn't scared of *him*, not one bit. He moved forward, slowly, baring his teeth like old Patch when you got him into a corner. "You *what*?" he repeated.

Rhys started walking backwards, head still held up, staring Brad straight in the eyes.

"I said, you've got a big mouth on you, and one day you're going to run out of things to scare me with."

Brad was almost silenced, but of course he wasn't really. "Oh yes, am I? You know, you're going to be really, really sorry you said that."

Still Rhys walked backwards, facing him. For some reason Brad was finding this disconcerting.

And then finally Rhys turned, and started to walk quickly up the lane, his yellow anorak glowing against the grey. For a moment, Brad didn't know how to react, then common sense kicked in and he ran and caught him up. For a few yards the boys walked alongside each other, silently, as though they were mates.

Then they turned into the bend, the hidden bend where no-one could see what you got up to.

On the left, far as you could see, were Williams' fields, fat and flowing, going on right up into the misty hill, a few Texels grazing peacefully, dingy against the silvered grass.

On the other side, falling down to the stream and the lake that gleamed at the foot, was the Cae, left useless by that woman, just overgrown with wild flowers in the spring, the one bit of land round here that wasn't Williams', and damn well ought to be, it wasn't right. Dad had offered her money, maybe not enough, but he wasn't going to pay the old witch more than it was worth. He was waiting, and one day, maybe when she was poor enough, he'd hit the right price and buy her out.

And then buy that miserable cottage of hers, and pull it down, or turn it into a holiday let, get fools from the cities to stay there at exorbitant rates, Brad's mum could do all the cleaning and whatnot, look after it, money for old rope…

It just wasn't right that folk who didn't deserve it should hang on to property other folk could make something out of.

Brad clamped his hand now on Rhys's shoulder, feeling the paltry little bones of shoulder blade and arm beneath his meaty grip. For he had an idea now, something that would make the kid really squirm, really wet himself.

"You and me," he said, softly still, "you and me is going for a little walk." And he turned the unresisting lad right round to the metal gate that led down to the Cae. He undid the gate with one hand, shoved it open with a clang.

The grass was slippery and made them both skid a bit, but Brad's force overcame that as he impelled Rhys downwards, their footsteps making a green trail in the frosty grass.

And at the foot of the meadow, clumps of reed and water grasses, and the still gleaming surface of the lake. Frozen it was, too, a light skim of ice stretched over the top, and below you could see depths of a weird green blackness that seemed to go down for ever, though he knew that the lake must only be a few feet deep.

For no reason at all, Brad felt himself shiver. And now he remembered, surely there were other stories about the lake, as well as the girl who drowned herself there. What were they? His gran had been full of them, but he never listened to her much anyway. But now fragments of those stories came back to him. Unexplained things, folk who wouldn't go near, folk who'd been and come back changed, folk who got bad dreams. He couldn't remember details now, but still enough to make him feel like a goose just walked over his grave.

Still, he wasn't going to let the lad see that. "Awright now," he said. "And what about you going for a little swim?"

And he grabbed the back of the boy's puny neck, and pushed him forward, into reeds and frozen mud. Of course he wasn't going to do it straightaway, had to get a bit of fun first, had to make the boy really afraid, so that he'd get the most out of the thing when it really happened.

"Cold and wet down there," he hissed into the boy's ear. "Wonder how long you'd last without breathing?

Minute? Half minute? Not long, anyway, and they'd find your body there tomorrow morning, poor lad, must have gone down there on his way home, and slipped, couldn't nothing be done, that's what they'd find."

The boy jerked his head upwards suddenly, almost dislodging Brad's hand. "They'd find two sets of footsteps leading down," he said. "That's what they'd find."

This wasn't going right, not right at all.

But you didn't stop Brad Williams just like that! "Cold and wet," he went on, "and filthy tasting too, I bet, wriggly things swimming right into your mouth, couldn't stop them, could you?"

The kid was still squirming, and somehow managed to twist himself again, flinging his head back. "You'd be surprised what I can do, Brad Williams," he gasped. "Always called my mum a witch, didn't you, well, you see just what a witch's brat can do!"

And from somewhere the little runt found a way of pulling right out of Brad's grasp, and uprighting himself, so that it was Brad who stumbled and almost slipped into reeds and mud.

Just because the ground was so slippery, that's all it was. He'd get his balance again in a minute.

But he didn't. Almost as though his legs wouldn't move, he was stuck there on the muddy slippery edge, trying to stop himself lurching right forward into the lake…

…the icy surface, that now seemed to have got thicker and more shining, the black depths almost glowing beneath it Then something seemed to break through, just below the glassy surface…

Bloody hell! It was a *girl*! A girl's face looking right up at him out of the water, flattened beneath the ice.

He could see open dark eyes, the dark hole of an opened mouth, the whiteness of her skin, and the dark tendrils of hair that floated and waved beneath the surface.

Almost as though she was trying to cry out under the ice. But the face didn't look scared. It looked… angry.

And suddenly he could feel something on the back of his neck, the boy's bird-like claw holding him tightly and then pitching him forward.

He threw out arms to stop himself, but it was no good. Something seemed to come up at him right out of the water, something long and wavy like an octopus's tentacle, only this had a girl's hand at the end...

And it gripped him around the back of his neck, harder than anyone had ever held him before, and pulled him down.

He could feel the cold coming off the icy surface as he fell, feel the impact as his face smashed against it, and amid shards of icy cold was pulled further and further down, so that the shock of the freezing water hit him with a great smack in the face. Then below that and below still, and because he hadn't had time to take a breath before he was pitched in, he knew that he wasn't going to be able to breathe for much longer.

His lungs hurt, his chest, his head pounded, his ears drummed. As his mouth opened, he could feel the foul taste rushing in and wriggling things rushing in too...

And her face, that white open-mouthed face just below his, and now she seemed to be laughing.

His arms, still above the ice, flailed uselessly on the hard glassy surface. Something seemed to be holding his legs in a vice.

His head was bursting. His eyes were going to pop out of his head, his heart had swelled to a huge size, and then there was just blackness, blackness and pain, and he felt his whole consciousness starting to go and the life was being pulled from him…

Then suddenly it was all over. The force that had been holding his legs down now tugged him out, so that his head came juggling and lurching out of the ice, and the brightness flooded his eyes.

He fell face down on the wet grass while the water gushed and bubbled out of his mouth, his nose. He was sick, throat-raspingly sick all over the grass. Then at last he managed to sit up, trembling all over.

He stood up, slowly. He looked around. The kid was standing there, looking at him thoughtfully, swinging his school bag, a few feet away. He said, "You really didn't ought to have done that, Bradley Williams."

Then he was off, hurrying up the hillside slope to the big metal gate.

Brad brushed down his soaking hair, now feeling as if it was turning to ice. His fleece was soaking and covered with bits of weed, and stained down the front where he'd thrown up. He could smell his own sick.

He turned to look at the water, expecting to see thick ice, and the hole where he'd fallen.

But there was no thick ice, only a thin wrinkled skin on the surface, unbroken. No girl's face, no open mouth, no waving hair.

Only, as he slowly tried to pull himself together, and make his way, trembling and shaking up the hill, dragging his school bag, he was sure he could hear the sound of someone, or something, laughing at him.

A DOG IS FOR LIFE

Catherine Butler

"Every misfortune is an opportunity in disguise," said Lucy Wilkes.

That's Lucy all over. She's bright and bonnie and bounce-back optimistic, like a rubber ball that misses the lampshade and hits you in the eye on the rebound. We've been friends for years, but I'm glad I don't sit next to her in every class.

When Lucy's cat Fudge was killed last October she was upset, of course, but even while she was reaching for the Kleenex she was thinking how to turn the situation to her advantage. From that day on she started pestering her parents for a dog, quietly but persistently. She's an expert at that.

"It will – it *might* – help put the bad memories behind me," she'd tell them, her voice just shy of a whimper.

By late November they looked about ready to give in, and I don't blame them. Of course they wanted to make it right. What parent wouldn't, after what happened to poor Fudge? It had taken days just to get the blood stains out of the lawn.

In a way I admired Lucy, but I was a little sickened, too. It wasn't just that she seemed a bit quick to forget Fudge (even if he was a scraggy old mog who spent twenty hours of every day asleep on the sofa). More important, wanting a dog had been my idea, my *thing*, and now Lucy was taking it over. It didn't help that the chances of my parents buying *me* a dog were nil. When I mentioned it at breakfast one morning – weeks before copy-cat Lucy – they swung into their double-act as if they'd been rehearsing.

"It would need walking every day," was Dad's opening move.

"It would be alone in the house," said Mum.

"The vet's bills!" exclaimed Dad, looking to heaven.

"I'd walk it! I'd look after it! I'd save all my pocket money!" I told them. "I always keep my promises, you know that!" But whatever promises I made they were ready with more objections, a never-ending supply.

So, when I was at Lucy's after school that day, and her mum started dropping hints about how Christmas was coming up, and Lucy shot me a smug look across her fish and chips – well, of course I felt hard done by. And when she went on about it afterwards, wondering what name to choose and whether she'd like a terrier or a spaniel better – well, of course there was going to be a row. And after that – Okay, it was childish to refuse her dad's offer of a lift home, but I had my dignity to think of. I turned on my heel, and set off into the November evening alone.

It was only eight o'clock, and the walk was along a well-lit road, but I felt foolish as soon as I turned the corner from Lucy's. The sky was cloudless, and that made me feel more exposed, somehow, there in the empty street. I quickened my pace a little. A big moon bobbed along the sports centre roof as I passed. The moon is always bigger in winter, I've noticed. It comes into its kingdom then. It has fancy titles, too: the butter-yellow Harvest Moon; the Hunter's Moon, wakeful and unblinking; and last of all the famished Wolf Moon, gnawing at the year's end.

Last time I'd walked from Lucy's, a few weeks earlier, the fat moon of harvest had been shining. It occurred to me now with a shudder that it must have been the very night when Fudge –

I did my best to stop the thought in its tracks. I didn't like to imagine what I might have been sharing the streets with, the night Lucy's cat died.

"Wait up, Nell!"

I jumped, at the male voice behind me. But it was only my big brother Adam, running to catch up. I'd not recognized him in the dark.

Not that Adam looked exactly safe, with his hoodie and trainers. More like somebody's nightmare of a modern teenager.

"You shouldn't be on your own in the dark. It's dangerous. There's people like me about."

Had he read my mind? I was glad he'd turned up, anyway.

"It's only just gone eight," I grumbled.

"You're the boss. But let's walk together, yeah?"

His phone rang almost at once, and he moved a few paces ahead. "What's up?" he said, and fell into a muttered conversation that sounded like a conspiracy even to me.

That was the trouble with Adam. He really *had* been a bad lad, once. A couple of years ago he'd been part of a gang, and he'd begun to drift away from me, Mum and Dad, into a very dark place. A bit of vandalism here, a fight there, carrying a few messages, babysitting a package or two. Eventually, he went too far. I remember the night that policewoman came round to the house. Adam had spat in the custody sergeant's face, she told Mum and Dad.

"He's a got a vicious streak, that one. You ought to muzzle him."

We didn't talk about it afterwards, because we knew it couldn't be true – even though we also knew it *was*. Mum's an accountant, Dad works in marketing, and Adam was a well brought up boy on course for eight GCSEs. Surely he wasn't the type to take pot shots at pets with an air rifle, or key the new cars in the showroom forecourt? He must have been misled, my parents decided. There was an appearance at the Youth Court, with Adam every inch the respectable citizen in his tie and white shirt, full of scripted remorse. It must have done the trick, because he got no more than a fine and a few weekends helping out in the local park. We all did our best to forget about it. My parents moved Adam to a different school, and it was there he discovered his love for competitive running.

Mum and Dad were delighted, especially when he started winning trophies. A much better use for all that teenage energy, they agreed. The old Adam had been left in the dust.

But I couldn't relax. Adam was a good big brother – he looked out for me – but I didn't exactly trust him. Or rather – it's just that, seeing him move round the room you could sense the muscles under his skin, spring-loaded and powerful, and it was like watching a rider try to control a horse that's too strong for him. You never knew when he was going to buck – or bolt – or bite.

* * *

It must have been a fox that killed Fudge, Lucy's mum had said. There'd been bite marks on the body. But what kind of fox takes a cat's head clean off and leaves its body neatly spread-eagled on the lawn?

A fox with thumbs and eight fingers, that's what.

* * *

Adam walked me back to our house that night, but he didn't stay. His mate on the phone was calling him away, Adam wouldn't say where.

"Tell Mum not to wait up," he told me. "I'll be back by midnight."

He had college next morning, so I had a good idea how that would go down. Mum did wait up, of course, and Adam didn't come home till well after twelve, of course. I heard them rowing downstairs.

"I told you, I was watching a movie at Dexy's!" Adam shouted. "His uncle was with us! Phone him now, if you don't believe me." I could pretty much hear him thrusting the phone at her. "He's on speed dial!"

He knew she would never phone at that time of night – and by morning, what would be the point? I heard her and Dad talking in bed later, though. Mum was crying – the kind of half-quiet weeping that's louder because you're trying to hide it.

It's hard to say when I first knew something was badly wrong. Part of me guessed long before I could face it head on. Dark thoughts were gathering at the window, tap-tap-tap, and in the end I had to let them in.

Let's just say that I'd been waiting up for Adam too.

* * *

The next morning I was out of bed early. It was still dark when I let myself into the garden. The frost was so sharp I mistook it for snow. I left my footprints in the grass as I walked to the spot where Adam had vaulted the fence the night before. He could have walked up the path like any normal person, but he'd erupted with a yelp, over the fence and onto the lawn. I'd seen it clearly from my window. He'd looked as if he'd been running, but that wasn't necessarily suspicious. After all, running was what he did best.

I moved to the rose bush near the shed, wary of the thorns. That was where he'd thrown something the night before – carelessly, like a toy he'd grown tired of. A round object, about the size of a cricket ball.

It didn't take long to find it, frosted and tangled with the woody stems of the roses. I didn't want to pick it up, but I made myself.

It had been part of a tabby cat, once. The markings were still visible beneath the gloops of frozen blood and spit. A little stub of ear poked up, and the jaw hung loose. I don't know what had become of the body – perhaps it was spread-eagled on a lawn somewhere? – but there was no doubt that Adam had come home last night carrying a severed head.

Mum did not wait up the next night, or the night after that. But I did. I saw the Hunter's Moon rise and prowl across the sky, breaking cover from the thin clouds. I saw the lawn turn ghostly as the night frost bit. And I saw Adam return in the small hours both times – never by the front gate, always prickling with energy, always streaked with dark. When I slept, I dreamed of sharp teeth and matted hair.

I could not face another night like that.

It was already getting dark when I walked into his

room without knocking. That was a crime in itself, of course. Teenage boys' rooms were private; you never knew what you were going to find.

Adam was eating a ham and ketchup sandwich, messily. "What do you want, Nell?"

"Mum asked me to bring your plate down, if you've finished with it," I improvised. "How's the training?"

"Good." He licked his fingers clean. "Been going for some long runs."

I sat on the bed, and said in what I hoped was a casual voice, "You shouldn't overdo it. You're not getting enough sleep."

He scowled. "I sleep just fine."

"You got in at three this morning. You kept it quiet, but I heard."

"What if I did? What's it to you, Nell?" Suddenly he was hostile and suspicious. Ketchup was leaking from the sandwich as he gripped it. Disgusting.

"I'm just worried about you," I said weakly.

"Thanks, but when I need a babysitter I'll let you know. All right?"

That *was* ketchup, wasn't it?

"See you later, Nell." He reached for his headphones.

I yelped out: "What happened to Lucy's cat?"

I hadn't meant to ask out of the blue like that, but the words jumped off my tongue.

He looked startled for a moment, but then he gazed back at me very steadily: "What did you say?"

"Can you swear you had nothing to do with what happened to her cat? Or the others since then? Have you and your mates been playing some kind of sick game?"

"I've no idea what you're talking about," he said, almost lazily, as if he didn't expect to be believed and was past caring.

"I thought you were over all that stuff. Killing cats and squirrels. You're better than that."

"Yeah, right, I'm *so* much better than that."

"Of course you are! You ran four hundred metres in less than fifty seconds last summer. You're the best in the school! You should take some pride in yourself." I must have sounded like our mother. "There's no point in denying it, Adam. I saw you drop this in the garden." I set what was left of the tabby's head on his plate, next to what was left of the sandwich. "Do you really think it's a laugh to catch somebody's pet and set a Staffy on it?"

"It wasn't a Staffy," he said quietly, gazing at the cat.

"I don't care what breed it was! You still had a dog ripping a cat to pieces!"

His voice was low and hollow, without expression: "Listen, Nell. It – wasn't a dog."

It took a few seconds for those words to sink it. I realised then how hard I'd been hoping I was wrong. Hoping against hope that it *was* a dog.

He saw my expression, then looked away, disgusted. "But you don't need to worry your head about it. You're a girl."

Now, *that* was offensive. "I can understand anything you can, you pig!"

"That's not what I mean! Girls aren't affected. It's not your problem."

"I *am* affected, Adam. I'm scared stiff! Hadn't you noticed?"

"Okay, Scooby Doo. So, what exactly are you scared of? What do you *think* is going on?"

A horrified embarrassment clamped my mouth shut. *You can't unsay it, once it's said.* Outside, the Hunter's Moon had risen. I stared it full in the face, and it stared back at me.

"What's the matter? Cat got your tongue?"

"Last night," I began, as steadily as I could, "you sneaked back into your room by climbing on the shed roof and in through the window, the way you used to when you were… wild. I couldn't believe what I was seeing, at first. Your face – "

"What about my face?" His voice was low in the throat.

"Not just your face. The blood was everywhere. All over your hands and shirt. That Gorillaz T you wear all the time? That was drenched. Where is it now, Adam? Not in the wash – I've checked."

"I'm not into Gorillaz any more."

"So where did that blood come from? And don't change the subject. You can't hide the truth from me for ever."

Adam sighed, deep and long. It seemed to tremble through his entire body. "You've got it the wrong way around, Nell," he said at last. "Mum and Dad and me – we haven't been hiding the truth from you. We've been sheltering *you* from the truth. Believe me, there's a difference."

The way he said it – I've never heard anyone sound so lonely. I wanted to hug him. I wanted to run for my life.

"But you're right," he said. "It's too late for pretending. The change has gone too far: no one can stop it now. There've been others in our family, way back, and the story's always the same. It only happens to boys. You seem to be normal till you hit sixteen, and then... you're not. Nell, each month sucks more of the human from me. By the time the Wolf Moon comes, there won't be much left."

He beckoned me to him.

"Close your eyes, Nell, and touch my face." He saw me flinch, and grabbed my wrist. "*Do it.*"

So I closed my eyes. As soon as I did, the touch of his hand upon my wrist seemed to change. It no longer felt like Adam. This grip was sinewy, coarse, with tapered nails that dug into my skin. It was strong, too, as it guided my fingers to his face. I felt the stubble of his cheek. Then I realised that it was not stubble after all. My fingers were moving over thick, bristly hair. Where his nose should be they found a muzzle, with a wet snout at its end. And beneath that...

I opened my eyes, wide.

"All the better to eat you with," said Adam sadly.

* * *

Lucy got a dog that Christmas, just as she'd wanted. It turns out that her parents had put their name down for a floppy-eared spaniel at the Rescue Centre. It was like a china dog come to life, Lucy told me later. So they weren't too pleased to find an unexpected visitor on their back doorstep, three nights before Christmas Eve. A large dog with thick, grizzled hair, white by the light of the Wolf Moon. Lucy loved it on sight.

"It's so *big*," Lucy's mother complained to mine. "I don't have time to walk a dog that size. Lucy says she will, but we'll see how long *that* lasts."

He is big, too. When he growls, it's like someone fired up a chainsaw somewhere deep inside his throat. And you should see him run! There's a bit of husky in him, Lucy thinks, but more Alsatian. He'll win no prizes at Cruft's but he's beautiful, with brown eyes that look back at you in a way even Lucy's mum says is almost human. They call him Merlin.

I talk to him when Lucy's out of the room.

"Adam?" I say. "It *is* you, isn't it?"

His tail slaps the lino, though he cannot speak. What does *that* mean?

"I'm so sorry, Adam. I wish I'd known sooner. Maybe we could have done – something – "

I choke on the words I don't have. It sounds pathetic, I realise. I'm almost glad he can't reply. Anything Adam had to say would be sarcastic. But dogs don't do sarcasm.

At first I wondered why he attached himself to Lucy's family, not ours. I resented it, to be honest. Then I saw how difficult it would have been. No teenage boy wants to be taken for walks by his little sister. Besides, no one could love a dog more than Lucy loves him. She really did want a pet as much as she had said.

Oh, but I miss my brother.

I spend a lot of time at Lucy's house these days. Mine isn't much fun, since Adam went missing. Christmas got cancelled, pretty much. Mum and Dad keep up the pretence even now, months later. They wonder aloud where Adam might be, and phone the Family Liaison Officer every week in case of news. I suppose they think they're still protecting me. I can't stand it.

I won't tell Lucy the truth, though. Adam has a good life, and I don't want to spoil things for either of them. And that, I suppose, is how this story ends. You might even call it a happy ending, looked at in the right light. Or perhaps not so happy after all. Either way, for better or worse they're together, and not just for Christmas.

For them, more than for anyone, a dog is for life.

HOME FOR THE HOLIDAYS

Rhiannon Lassiter

Lazy as a sunbeam I wander through the meadows in the dying days of summer. My bare feet sink into the warm brown earth. The fields are gold and green and buzzing with butterflies and bees. The sky is an azure bowl upended over the world.

I wind white water lilies into a chain and plait them into my sun-streaked hair. My dress is white muslin, simple as a shroud. Beneath it my skin is nut brown, hot and dry.

High in the dome of the sky a black bird wheels and I shiver, goosebumps rising on my skin, seeing that predatory shadow.

This was where it all began, here in the water meadows. Imagine us seen from above, maidens scattered through the greenery like the wildflowers we are gathering, our hair and clothes bright and festive. The watcher descends, a long slow swoop, taking time to pick his target.

I am the target. Unwary, oblivious, innocent. In my memory the dark shape falls from above, the earth splits open beneath my feet, my mouth opens in an O and a scream escapes as I am caught.

This is where my story begins. Perhaps you already know how it must end.

Now the memories pale in the flood of sunshine, the distant shadow is cleared from the sky, I am alone in the fields. I choose to leave the river bank, walking through the stubbled fields where the short stalks lash my ankles and prickle my feet.

Fruit hangs heavy in the vineyards and orchards, dragging down the vines and boughs. My mother is waiting for me under the trees. She is Demeter, the goddess of fertility. She is larger than life, glowing with health and vitality. She reaches out to claim me and twines her strong brown arms around my neck. She strokes my hair, gathering it through her hands like harvest wheat.

"It's so good to have you here," she says. "Do you see how happy everyone is when you're home? You make us happy."

She speaks as though it is my choice to stay, to leave, to bestow happiness like a gift. She speaks as though a whistle will summon me home – and so it will. But when summer ends it won't be her tune I dance to.

In the fields farmers bring home the harvest. Children chase each other through the maize and the older ones play games at the edge of the woods that are just becoming dangerous.

I watch as a young shepherd boy chases a nymph into a grove of cherry trees, bearing down on her until they fall laughing together into a drift of leaves. Their bodies intertwine and I turn away. The games of kiss chase are all part of the late summer madness that falls over everyone. It's only me who sees the shadow of the trees and the drift of leaves as sinister. The shepherd and the nymph leave the grove hand in hand, leaning on each other.

Girls flare suddenly into womanhood, a harvest to be gathered. One second a child, a clocktick later a nubile nymph; suddenly part of someone else's story. Heroic men reach out and take.

The trees are aflame with autumn colours: the red of burning coals, orange tongues of fire, scorched yellow. I wear a crown of golden leaves at the harvest dances: spinning and whirling like a leaf in the wind. The peasant girls and nymphs form rings around me. The boys and men dance circles around us.

Food is abundant. All the fruits of the field and the orchard are spread in a feast. Apples, pears, wild cherries; plums the colour of bruises; melons ripe and succulent – but no pomegranates.

My mother is seated at the head of the high table, presiding over the festival. Her clothing is wine red and beaten gold and the women around her sink down in awe when she looks at them. Demeter is Queen of the Summer and her smiles fall like rays across the company.

When the black god hid me under the earth she roamed the earth in quest of me, a madwoman calling constantly for her lost child. Famine followed in her footsteps. The earth was barren as an empty womb. All creation cried out for succour but Demeter cared for nothing but the daughter she had lost. In the end the Great Gods were forced to intervene to save humanity – but too late to save me.

Now at the harvest dance Demeter seems radiant with joy. She is surrounded by her worshippers, she has her daughter once again, these are her rites that are celebrated. Am I the only one who sees it cannot last? Children grow up, belief fails as doubts are sown, and I am not the same girl who was snatched from the wildflower meadow. For half a year he held me hostage. Demeter chooses to forget, but I don't have that luxury.

The harvest cups run red with ruby wine. Faces are flushed with it, speech slurred, eyes brightened – or dulled. As the music becomes wilder and the drink stronger, Dionysus arrives with his company: goat-footed men and loose-limbed women with satirical smiles.

I eat bread soaked in honey mead. My lips are

sticky with it: my body heavy with the drug. The God of Wine catches me around the waist, daring where others dare not.

"Is it Persephone or Kore?" he asks. "Or Melindia or Hagne or Despoina?" His right hand tangles in my hair while his left draws me closer to his body. "How old are you now, anyway?"

"Old enough to be married," I remind him and his hands drop away like dead leaves.

At the edge of the company I stand apart, the woods at my back as I watch the revelry. In Spring the nymphs and dryads danced among the green buds and white blossom around a slender stem of an olive tree hung with laurel. Now it's Autumn and they dance again in drifts of fallen leaves around a blazing fire.

It's my story they are telling in the beat of drums and the rhythmic pounding of feet. It's my return they celebrate in springtime and my departure they grieve in the fall.

My story – but it doesn't feel as though it belongs to me. Perhaps because they never asked for my version. Our poets, like our heroes, are men – and it does not occur to them to ask.

It seems distant; a myth of long ago, a story with an ending everyone knows, a closed book. I draw away, under the shadow of the trees, the warmth of the fire at my back. These last few weeks whenever my mother sees me at the edge of the woods she comes running, her hair streaming behind her like a banner, her dress dishevelled into a flag of despair. She clutches at my hands, my feet, rocking me with her body, keeping me rooted to the earth.

Her moans and cries mean that she loves me. But what is love but the desire to have and to hold? She says that his love is only passion, possession, power. I have not told her he says the same of her.

The wind whistles: a shrill chilly sound that echoes through the forest. The trees shake their branches, casting their rustling garments to the ground to emerge stripped bare and skeletal. The dead leaves catch in my hair, dry and crackling. I step into the shadow of the wraith wood.

I am not sure if I am following a path or if the path is created as I walk. Beneath my feet the earth is cold and rimed with frost. The forest is ghostly, half-glimpsed shapes slip in and out of the shadows. The rustle of leaves, the crackle of dead twigs, the moan of the wind: they whisper to me, speaking of subjects that summer cannot know.

There are stones on the road, sharp-edged flints that slice my feet. If I looked back would I see a trail of my own blood? But I do not look back.

I have walked this road before, in both directions. I know what lies at either end.

The road is steeper too. The trees thin down as the hillside rises, their trunks stunted or twisted against the battering onslaught of a cold wind. Above, the countenance of the sky is dark and stormy, frowning down at me.

A flurry of snow casts itself into the air, dusting my hair with ice crystals, chilling my skin and damping my dress. A freezing fog descends and the mountain steps spill gravel and hailstones in a rattling hammering scree. I brace myself against the storm, needles of frost stab down from the sky and are whipped away by the wailing wind. My face is reddened with the slap and sting of the cold. My lips are numb with its kisses.

Night is falling, like a black god descending through the heavens. It is a winter night, cold and bleak and terrible. Spring is a long-gone memory, distant as childhood. Summer is erased as though it never was. Autumn has been left behind. Now there is only the stark face of night, the burning eyes of the stars, the world a blank page on which winter has written his name.

Ahead a black mouth yawns open in the hollow hill. The stone road leads through it: a lane to the land of the dead. Still my footsteps do not falter. There is nowhere to go but forward.

As I descend into the dark, the stone walls close in over and around me with a cold heavy embrace. Down into the depths, where the light dwindles and life decays, into the land of husks and rinds.

The first time I came this way was not so easy, no smooth passageway, no open road. Caught in the thunderous embrace of the lord of the underworld the earth shook and burst apart, a chasm opened, the swoop became a plunge, the air screamed past and we fell together into the dark.

This time I am granted the illusion of choice. The road winds slowly down into the mountain, taking its time, secure in the inevitability of its own ending.

I am alone on the road. But beside and behind me I hear the scrape of scales on stone, paws padding, insectine legs clacking and clicketing in a sudden scurry of movement. Leathery wings flap overhead, moths blunder blindly across my face kissing me with dust, webs cling and tangle in my hair.

The light is dying but this is a path I could walk blindfold. Emptiness gapes around me, the path thins down to a thread unreeling through the void of blackness. My steps are sure on the span of stone across the dizzying depths of the abyss.

I can hear water dripping, the trickle growing to a flow, drawn down as I am into the dark.

Acheron is the river of sorrow, it flows with the salt water of tears, the clay bed red as tear-stung eyes. Cocytus is named for lamentation, a howling waterfall that hurls itself from stone to stone, careless of itself as it plunges down. Phlegethon is a river of fire, the world broken open, as molten stone rages along well grooved channels.

The waters of Lethe are black. This is the river of forgetfulness. No mortal leaves the underworld without drinking from that river. Would they return to the wheel of birth and suffering if they recalled how it must end? Who would willingly enter Hades?

At last we come to the river of hate: the Styx.

The ferryman is waiting. He expects nothing from me and receives nothing; we exchange no words or glances. I step into the boat and cold coins stamp themselves into the soles of my feet. The faces of kings lie blindly staring, tarnish creeping over their proud visages, an indistinguishable army of forgotten empires.

The water is flowing slowly and inevitably. The oar enters the water, the boat slides, the oar lifts and falls again. There are no lilies, only waving weeds, reaching up from below to seize and trap and tangle the unwary traveller. Strange that you must pay to enter a realm that is so loath to let you go.

On one side of the river the shore is empty, on the other multitudes of ghosts wander listlessly through the dead lands. In life they were heroes, their story one of action and adventure, the world shaped by the choices they made. But now they have come to the end of choices and decisions. The scent of sacrifices drifts to them from the living world, blood quickening briefly with remembered lusts and passions, the incense drifts past and the memories die.

This is the end all must come to. Is it worse to come to it from a life where you were the actor or one where you were acted on? For the heroes this is the ultimate dread. But when were their wives and daughters ever anything but lambs to be shepherded or sacrificed? No women wander in the wasteland. What fear can the loss of power hold for those who were ever powerless?

But what power do any of us have whose lives are determined by the actions of the High Gods? Compared to them all lesser beings are as mayflies. Heroes shine in their hour of glory. Kings stamp their face on the world. Demigods rise to notice for their deeds. But in the end everything falls beneath the sway of the three sons of the Titans: Zeus, Poseidon and Hades.

Between them they divided up the sky, the sea and the land of shades. Who received the greatest portion? All that is born must die.

The boat arrives on the far beach and I step on to the shore.

The sand is white and gritty, ground from bone. Larger bones are flotsam scattered across the beach: the spines of fish, the ribs of animals, the arm and thigh bones of men. I walk through a cathedral arch of whalebone and am swallowed by the land of the dead.

The road is dusty and dry. The air is still.

Three roads converge at a crossroads. Hecate, the witch, curtsies to me. Three-faced, serpent-tongued, dressed in darkness. She bows to me, the Summer Girl, with baleful eyes and a jealous sneer.

Hecate is the goddess of boundaries and meetings. Perhaps I should have prayed to her as I was dragged across the line between life and death. Would she have answered my prayers, I wonder. Would she have fought for me as fiercely as Summer and Winter fought over me? My story ends in other people's choices. Half a daughter, half a wife. My boundary runs across the world like a scar.

I don't weep at the crossroads. Any tears I shed were lost in Acheron long ago. I don't wait for judgement. I have been judged and portioned.

The last road, the final road, leads to the Castle of Bone. Its ramparts loom before me. The phantoms that have padded and skirted behind me all this way resolve out of the gloom. To my left a monstrous three-headed hound paces alongside me. Its slavering jaws drip blood and foam and saliva, its hair bristles like porcupine quills and fragments of flesh cling to its claws.

Cerberus turns his horrible heads towards me, alert for my command. I have no desire he can fulfil but I allow him to walk in my shadow as we approach the last gate of hell.

Skeletons bow down to me. Demons fold their wings. Horrors do me homage. I walk through their midst and they draw back. Here at the heart of darkness the only light comes from me. The glow of gold from my hair, silver from my skin, bronze from my dress: the currency that summer pays to winter.

The walls are stone and bone. The floors are bone and stone. The ceiling is a black void extending upwards to infinity. All is lifeless, dead, unchanging. Empty.

All but the orchard garden, a tangle of vines and trees, an oasis in the darkness: a grove of pomegranate trees. In the underworld, in the deadlands, this copse of greenery exists in mocking contrast to the bonegarden.

I reach out and my hand closes around a fruit, feeling the resistance as I twist it from its parent stem.

It is soft and warm in my hand, a small red sun in the dark land.

After my abduction the days lengthened into weeks, the weeks cast a long shadow into months and I began to fear that years might pass in that unchanging empty land. The Fates themselves had ruled that anyone who ate or drank in the underworld must remain there forever. When the minions of the deadlands brought me their delicacies I pressed my lips shut and shook my head.

Then the lord of the underworld brought me a pomegranate, my favourite fruit. A familiar taste and scent and touch, a little round world of my own.

What power these little globes hold. A woman eats a fruit and the world changes. Was it greed or did a serpent tempt her? One bite of the fruit, four seeds, and she is complicit in her own disaster.

When it was revealed that I had eaten those four pomegranate seeds, Zeus determined that I must spend a quarter of the year underground in payment. From then on I would not belong to myself but to my story: daughter of summer, bride of winter, a shuttle on the loom of fate.

My white teeth bite into the sweet flesh. What harm can come to me now? I could strip the orchard bare and gorge myself sick on pomegranates if I wished. I spit the seeds on to the cold earth.

I enter the Hall of Hades. It is majestic, overpowering, threatening. The hosts of hell draw back from the red ribbon of my pathway, sheathing their claws and fangs and mandibles, folding their wings and closing their carapaces, their seething snakes and barking dogs quieting as I walk among them.

I draw my hands through my hair and away fall the flowers, the dead leaves, ice crystals, spiderwebs, bone dust and pomegranate blossom. My summer gold hair cloaks me, my skin glows honey sweet in the halls of bleached bone, my eyes are the blue of a clear and endless sky.

The wine velvet carpet is soft beneath my feet as I approach the throne. Cerberus pads past me to lie down at his master's feet. The host does not dance or sing or cry out but they are celebrating their own rituals in their own fashion.

He is waiting for me. He has waited an eternity, a season, a portion of a year. The winter king, the lord of the deadlands, the third son of the Titans. Hades. My husband.

His skin is pale as ashes, as dry as bone, as cold as ice. His body is a skeleton in a shroud of flesh – as is all that is mortal – a disguise for a god. He is clothed in shadow and smoke. His hair is raven black, his eyes are winter grey, his mouth is pale and bloodless.

Death claims all of us eventually. With black wings he stoops from the sky, lifts us from the earth and drags us away from home. Is it a sin to surrender when he will triumph either way? No one asked me my desires when they decided who would own me and how.

What if they asked me now? What would I say, what would I choose? No one ever does ask.

I think my mother is afraid to ask my about my life in the dead lands because she doesn't want to hear about the horror, the terror and the dread. She prefers pretence: a beautiful dream is better than an ugly reality.

My husband fears nothing, or so he would claim. But he does not ask either. I think he knows no woman would ever choose this desolation over the sunlight world above. Why else did he steal me? He could have come as a suitor. He could have asked – but he never asked and so I never said yes or no.

It is too late for choices. I am at the end of my story. My tale is told. The decisions made for me by distant powers. Still I ask myself the question. I ask it every season. If I could choose, what land would I call home? If love was mine to give, not theirs to take, where would I gift it and to whom?

I climb the steps to the dais. The host abases itself before us. I take my seat beside the dark lord.

He turns his skull-like visage towards me; his eyes are dark stars in the hollow sockets, his touch is as cold as the grave.

And his mouth tastes of pomegranates.

About the Contributors

Catherine Butler was born in Hampshire, where she grew up in a small market town near the New Forest. As a child, she spent most of her time wandering woods, trying to learn musical instruments, and learning about myths. She also loved reading ghost stories (both fictional and real) and scaring herself silly. Catherine now lives in Bristol, where she teaches English at a local university. As well as writing books for children and young adults, Catherine writes books about children's books. Some people think her obsessed. Her books (most of them published under the name Charles Butler) are fantasies, but they are fantasies set in our own world – or in worlds set at a slight, disconcerting angle to our own. They include *Calypso Dreaming*, *The Fetch of Mardy Watt*, *Death of a Ghost* and *The Lurkers*.

Susan Cooper wrote the classic five-book fantasy sequence *The Dark Is Rising*, in which one quiet little scene still scares people. She grew up in England but now lives in America, on an island in a Massachusetts saltmarsh. Besides novels and short stories, she has written screenplays and (just once, as co-author) a Broadway play. Her latest book for young adults is called *Ghost Hawk*, and yes, of course, there's a ghost in it.

Frances Hardinge was brought up in a sequence of small, sinister English villages, and spent a number of formative years living in a Gothic-looking, mouse-infested hilltop house in Kent. She studied English Language and Literature at Oxford, fell in love with the city's crazed, archaic beauty, and never found a good enough reason to leave.

Whilst working full time as a technical author for a software company she started writing her first children's novel, *Fly by Night*, and was with difficulty persuaded by a good friend to submit the manuscript to Macmillan. *Fly by Night* went on to win the Branford Boase Award, and was also shortlisted for the Guardian Children's Fiction Award. Her subsequent books, *Verdigris Deep*, *Gullstruck Island*, *Twilight Robbery* and *A Face Like Glass* are also aimed at children and young adults.

Frances is seldom seen without her hat and is addicted to volcanoes.

Katherine Langrish is the internationally published author of several children's fantasy novels including the Viking trilogy *Troll Fell*, *Troll Mill* and *Troll Blood* (HarperCollins), recommended in the School Library Association's 'Top 160 Books for Boys', republished in one volume as *West of the Moon*. Her fourth book, *Dark Angels* (US title *The Shadow Hunt*, HarperCollins) was listed as one of Kirkus Reviews' Best Books for Children 2010, and the US Board on Books for Young People's Outstanding International Books 2011. Her writing is strongly influenced by folklore and legends, and has often been compared with Alan Garner's. Katherine lives in Oxfordshire and is currently writing a two-part YA dystopia.

Rhiannon Lassiter is an author of science fiction, fantasy, contemporary, 'realist magicism', psychological horror and thriller novels for juniors, teenagers and young adults. She was born in 1977 and is the eldest daughter of award-winning children's author Mary Hoffman.

Rhiannon's first novel, *Hex*, was accepted for publication when she was nineteen years old. She completed the book and a sequel while at university reading English Literature at Corpus Christi College, Oxford.

Rhiannon has published eleven further novels, a non-fiction book about the supernatural and co-edited an anti-war anthology of poetry and prose, *Lines in the Sand*. Her psychological horror novel *Bad Blood* was nominated for six awards including the Guardian Prize and the BookTrust Prize. Her most recent novel, *Ghost of a Chance*, was published in February 2011.

Her favourite authors include Ursula LeGuin, Margaret Mahy and Octavia Butler. Her own novels explore themes of identity, change and becoming.

Rhiannon lives and works in Oxford, United Kingdom. Her ambition is to be the first writer-in-residence on the Moon.

Frances Thomas was born in Wales, but brought up in South London. She has written many books, including, for children, *I Found Your Diary* and *Polly's Running Away Book*. Her most recent adult book is a *A Bracelet of Bright Hair* and her biography of Christina Rossetti has also just been reissued. She has won the Tir na nOg prize four times for her children's books. Before she retired she used to also work as a teacher of dyslexic children. Now she lives with her husband in the middle of Wales.

Liz Williams is a science fiction and fantasy writer living in Glastonbury, England, where she is co-director of a witchcraft supply business. She is currently published by Bantam Spectra (US) and Tor Macmillan (UK), also Night Shade Press, and appears regularly in Realms of Fantasy, Asimov's and other magazines. She is the secretary of the Milford SF Writers' Workshop, and also teaches creative writing and the history of Science Fiction.